SOPHOMORE UNDERCOVER

SOPHOMORE UNDERCOVER

BEN ESCH

Disney · HYPERION BOOKS
New York

First Edition
1 3 5 7 9 10 8 6 4 2
Printed in the United States of America
Reinforced binding
Library of Congress Cataloging-in-Publication Data on file.
ISBN 978-1-4231-1303-4

Visit www.hyperionteens.com

For my Medici

SOPHOMORE UNDERCOVER

Chapter 1

Monday, 9:28 a.m.

"What the hell, Dixie?"

A piece of paper slammed against Dixie's computer screen, eclipsing the game of Ski Free that he'd been playing for the past hour. The paper, with a headline reading, HOMELESS MAN FOUND DEAD, was now stuck on the screen, fixed to the monitor by the magic of static electricity and the sugary glue of an RC Cola stain from the early nineties.

"Excuse me?" Dixie brushed the loose strands of hair off his forehead, ran his tongue along the smooth plastic of his retainer, and looked up in the general direction of his journalism teacher, Ms. Trasker ("Ms." as of eighteen months and one Hungarian yoga instructor ago). Though somewhere on the wrong side of forty-five, she was still attractive in a Glenn Close, masculine, frightening kind of way. So not so attractive at all, really.

But she was a woman, and sometimes that was enough.

At least for Dixie who had become enough of a man in his fourteen years to make the whole dance possible. In theory. His body's transition into adulthood had been a slow, uneven process, and Dixie was still unsure which parts were operating at full capacity. His face produced oil but, beyond a few dark patches on the sides of his mouth, no hair. His arms and legs sprouted out from the fabric borders of his clothes, though they gained none of the expected muscle tone or coordination.

Ms. Trasker's cheeks flared red as she pointed at the paper stuck to the computer screen. "This! What is this?"

Her voice ricocheted off the walls of the newspaper's small office. The space had previously been used as a darkroom for the photography department, until state health standards forced the reassignment of the room toward a less noxious chemical-dependent endeavor. However, there was still just enough room for a computer, a printer, and a verbally-abusive menopausal woman; and Dixie understood that was a solid enough foundation for any successful newspaper.

This was Dixie's elective period, and though most students used the time for study hall or model rocketry or any other excuse to get academic credit for napping or huffing rubber cement, Dixie decided to bolster his academic résumé by signing up for the school newspaper. As the most intelligent, dedicated, and only enrolled student in the class, he quickly became the lead reporter.

Dixie wiped the droplets of Trasker spit off his glasses. "That's my story, Ms—"

"No, I assigned you two hundred words to review the school play."

She did, and he went, but reconciling his secret admiration for Andrew Lloyd Webber with his discomfort around drama kids proved much too difficult to endure when Dixie sat down to write the article. That, and *Frasier* was on.

Oh, and there was the whole "homeless person overdose" thing he'd heard over the police scanner while his dad drove him to school that morning. Like Mel Nichols (journalism professor at Fresno State University, author of the textbook *Elementary Journalism*, and Dixie's personal and professional inspiration) said, "news is making priorities."

"This isn't a play review!"

Dixie's father was a cop. *Adoptive* father. *Second* adoptive father to be technical. His first adoptive father had been a figurative "bleeding heart" Berkeley professor, who became a literal bleeding heart Berkeley professor after a car crash two months into the adoption experiment.

The professor had no wife or children of his own, so custody was transferred to his closest living relative. And that's how, at the tender age of seven, Dixie came to live in the small mountain town of Stilton with Police Sergeant Dario Presto (second adoptive father), Mrs. Presto (first adoptive mother), and older brother, Brandon (first sibling of any kind to Dixie's knowledge).

"Pay attention!" Ms. Trasker struck the computer screen with her palm, rocking the bulky Macintosh just enough to knock the paper off the screen and onto the keyboard.

Dixie checked the progress of his skier: eaten by a yeti. At least he didn't hit a tree. That's how Sonny Bono died. So did a Kennedy. Wait. No, that was a bullet. Really not so much like a tree when he thought about it.

He looked back at Ms. Trasker and smiled; it was probably best to go with the soft sell on this one. "That's uhh . . . that's, you see, I decided to take the story in a different direction."

A rush of blood bottlenecked through Ms. Trasker's jugular. "A different direction? Do you know what week this is, Dixie?"

He looked down at his watch.

"Not the date, Dixie! It's homecoming week!" Ms. Trasker breathed deep and rubbed on her nicotine patch. "Homecoming week! You know that, right?"

He did. The cheery voices over the PA had told him so between the Pledge of Allegiance and the joke of the day ("What did the fish say when he hit the wall? Dam." Freaking hilarious.).

"I know."

"So why do you want me to put a story about a bunch of dead hobos in my homecoming edition?"

Dixie looked down at the pocket notebook on his desk and scanned through his notes for the story: drugs, death, mystery, transients. According to Nichols, it had all the elements of a "hard hitting" story. Well, the "transient" thing was a bit of a stretch, but front-page material, regardless. Besides, homecoming was completely retarded.

"Well, Nichols says that . . ."

"Screw Nichols!" Ms. Trasker slapped the computer monitor to punctuate her words. "We only use that piece-of-

6

crap book because the school can't afford anything better. He's a hack."

No, not Nichols, Dixie thought; all the man ever did was give.

"But it's the third overdose since the beginning of the school year. People might think it's important."

"Oh really? And I suppose that *people* would know better than the editor of a 1,200-circulation newspaper?"

Beyond serving as Ms. Trasker's favorite saying, that was also *technically* true. Twelve hundred students were enrolled at Stilton High School. Twelve hundred editions of the school paper, *The Stilton High Wildcat*, were photo-copied at the Kinko's. Twelve hundred newspapers were stacked on homeroom desks every second Friday. By third period, nine hundred were scattered across the quad, two hundred were in the trash, and fifty usually found themselves in the harder-to-reach nooks and crannies of the campus. That morning, Dixie had aimed at last week's sports section while using the urinal.

So that put the readership at about forty-one. But Ms. Trasker was still the editor in chief, and Dixie felt obligated to respect her judgment. Terror was also a factor.

"So you want me to write about homecoming, then?" Dixie asked.

"Only if you want to pass my class."

It was an empty threat but still got his attention. High marks were essential. Dixie liked to think of each grade point as getting another mile farther from Stilton to attend college. Currently, he was somewhere around Lubbock, Texas, and hoped to cross the Mason-Dixon Line by spring of his senior year.

Dixie blinked hard and readjusted his glasses. "Okay."

"Good, Dixie." Ms. Trasker put a hand on his shoulder. He suspected it was an attempt at affection. It had quite the opposite of the intended effect, but a sweet gesture regardless. "There's going to be a bonfire rally tomorrow night. I want two hundred words."

Five hundred meatheads dancing around a fire—that should lead to good things, Dixie thought; but what's another sexual harassment lawsuit for the sake of school spirit?

"What if there's another . . . you know, another overdose?"

The hand on Dixie's shoulder tightened. Hard. He stifled a whimper. He didn't want to get her overexcited. If he learned anything from Steinbeck, it was to tread lightly among those with strong grips and simple minds.

"Forget it."

"Good," Ms. Trasker said, and released his shoulder. "And I'm going to need your play review by sixth period."

Dixie nodded.

"And Dixie?"

"Yes, ma'am?"

"Be a dear and fetch me a cinnamon roll from the cafeteria."

Chapter 2

Monday, 1:26 p.m.

"Funt got tit-tay!"

Dixie was a sophomore, but thanks to a late birthday and some advanced testing in his early years (like a young Mozart with the kazoo, that kid) he would not turn fifteen until a few weeks into summer vacation.

It was difficult for Dixie to be both the youngest and the smallest boy in his class, but he took some solace in the fact that at least he'd be able to drive when he was a senior. All that left was finding a car, friends, and a shared destination for the two in the meantime.

He appreciated the extra time to figure it all out.

"Funt got tit-tay!"

Maybe he'd even have a cool mustache by then, too, but Dixie wasn't very optimistic. Asians didn't seem like a particularly furry people. Except for wispy beards. Those kung fu monks could really grow a beard.

"Tit-tay!"

Funt punched a locker and threw his football helmet against the wall. "Shut up, dickhead!"

There you go, Funt, Dixie thought; don't let them talk to you like that.

"Tit-tay!"

Funt really did have tit-tay, but besides the C-cups he looked normal enough. Levis. Adidas. Boobs. The all-American boy.

"Funt got tit-tay!"

The other jocks in the locker room joined in the chant. Just like every other day. It was probably quite relaxing for them before all that business of running into each other on the football field for the next few hours. Dixie didn't really care what they did, as long as they weren't messing with him.

That also happened. A lot. It was unavoidable, really—he was an intruder in their territory.

Dixie blamed the whole messy arrangement on Coach Hamm. The stupid bastard thought Dixie's last name, Nguyen (pronounced almost like "win"), started with W, and gave him the last pick of lockers. That meant sharing in the varsity room. With a jock. Not good times, especially during football season.

The same thing happened last year, and though the pattern suggested a deliberate attack, Coach Hamm didn't seem smart enough for such subtle cruelty. He probably just wasn't paying attention.

"Funt got tit-tay!"

Dixie's locker buddy, Rick, was also a sophomore, as

well as middle linebacker on the varsity football team, and the official starter of the daily "tit-tay" chant.

They didn't have much in common.

Beyond muscle mass, shoulder acne, and all-around disposition, the biggest distinction between the two was body hair: Rick had a carpet of blond fuzz in a droopy crescent around his lips, and tufts of yellow peeked out from the towel around his waist.

Such modesty was the exception. Most days Rick would parade around without his towel, balls free and swinging. That is, unless he was feeling particularly rambunctious. Then, he tucked his penis and scrotum between his legs and chased Dixie around the locker room while screaming that he was a girl. Rick called it the "Russian cootchie," and though the closest thing to a "cootchie" Dixie had yet encountered, the effort was not appreciated.

Of course, Dixie supposed the situation might not have been so intolerable if he didn't have to spend so much column space and creative output writing about these same idiots and celebrating their ability to hurl themselves into obese kids from neighboring towns. He didn't even need a thank-you. A day without getting his underwear yanked up through his "no touch" zone would have been gratitude enough.

So far, that hadn't happened.

"Hey, pixie dick." That was Rick's pet name for Dixie. "Don't bend over like that, you're lookin' kinda sexy."

"Sorry?" Dixie straightened his body against their shared locker. Lesson number One of locker room survival:

never present a target. So far it had only been wedgies, but . . .

"Don't apologize." Rick curled his lip up and around his fangs. "I like it."

Dixie lifted his shoe up against his inner thigh, and knotted the laces at double speed. Just one more lap around the bunny hole to go.

He looked up—the towel was still on Rick's waist, and everything was going to be fine, and . . .

Oh, dear Christ.

"Hey, Dixie, guess what? I'm a girl!"

And out came the Russian cootchie.

Dixie abandoned the bunny mid loop, grabbed his inhaler and pocket notebook from the locker, and sprinted for the door. He heard the slap of Rick's bare feet on the pavement closing in behind him, but his salvation was in sight—not even Rick had the gumption to pull off the Russian cootchie in front of the entire PE class. He pushed through the locker room doors and into the gymnasium. Rick did not. It was another day of survival.

Dixie was red and sweaty from the sudden exertion, and decided that he needed to ratchet up his cardiovascular routine if he intended to keep up this hunted-animal thing for the long term. Maybe start with the Tae Bo tapes again. That was a fun few weeks, and besides, it wasn't like his dad could think he was any more of a sissy.

Dixie tucked the notebook into the back of his gym shorts and secured it against the waistband. He never went anywhere without it. Sure, it made his ass lopsided and was uncomfortable during long periods of sitting, but like Nichols said, "most stories are lost in the time it takes to find paper and pencil" and he didn't want to be unprepared for any breaking stories.

"Line up!" Somehow, Coach Hamm slurred even while yelling.

The popular rumor was that Coach Hamm was an alcoholic, and though probably true, this explanation was far too simple for Dixie. No, the man's condition could only be caused by extensive paint huffing, or a long and unsuccessful career on the stick-fighting circuit.

"You too, Win!"

Dixie stepped into formation, shouted out his name for roll call, and began his daily ration of state mandated exercise.

He still felt an adrenaline charge from being chased by the naked linebacker and completed a set of pushups off his knees. It felt good. If he kept this up, he might even take off his T-shirt the next time he went to the public swimming pool. Modesty was for pussies.

Unfortunately, Dixie's newfound appreciation for physical fitness was sidetracked by a sudden tightness in his lower stomach. Whoops. In all the excitement of the locker room, Dixie forgot to stop for his scheduled afternoon movement.

Such deviation was unacceptable. Dixie hadn't spent so much time, energy, and fiber supplement disciplining his colon to let some naked gorilla compromise his routine.

So, while the rest of the class followed Coach Hamm

to the field for archery, Dixie sneaked back into the locker room.

Beyond varsity athletes and those with robust immune systems and low aesthetic standards, few people used the locker room lavatory. It wasn't surprising. The toilets flooded, the mirrors were covered in black marker diagrams of vaginas, and the walls were stuccoed with wads of wet toilet paper thrown during some celebration or another.

While the pervasive grossness of the place might have stopped a lesser man, Dixie was an expert at improvised bathroom sanitation. He didn't just rip out a wax paper seat cover and call it a day. That was for amateurs. Instead, he built a nest of toilet paper squares around the porcelain. Once for support, twice to be sure, three times for comfort, four times (and this was key) to prevent the more virulent strains of germs from climbing up into his system. Paranoid, maybe, but Dixie would much rather be twice careful than once leper.

Satisfied with the protection of his seat, Dixie sat down and started to hum the theme song to *Cheers*—but something threw off his concentration before any magic could happen.

"She's a slut."

People. In the bathroom. Dixie stopped humming and braced his feet against the stall door. He was at his most vulnerable and saw no point in surrendering his location.

"Dude, knock it off."

Two voices. Masculine. Dixie supposed that made sense.

"What? Why else are you dating her?" The first voice was abusive but didn't have enough screech to be Rick.

"She's hot."

"And she's a slut."

"That's just a rumor."

"Please, you freakin' said it yourself, man."

Dixie leaned forward to peek through the crack in the stall. The toilet paper muffled any joint creaks from the weight shift: another plus for the four-tissue plan. He wondered if Thomas Edison felt something like this. It was nice.

"Okay, so maybe that's what attracted me in the first place or whatever, but she's my girlfriend now, and you could stop being such a dick about the whole thing."

"Who's being a dick?"

Dixie couldn't see up to either of their faces, but the floppies under the shirt of the bigger one told him all he needed to know: that was Funt.

"You! You're being a dick."

The "dick" wore a matching blue sweatsuit with the fabric bunched at the knees. His legs were so pale that Dixie couldn't tell where sock stopped and skin began.

"What? I'm just pointing out that she's into sodomy. That's her problem, not mine."

Even with the unique pigmentation, Dixie didn't recognize the albino. That was a surprise; he didn't think such an interesting deviation in the school's genetic sample would have escaped his attention.

"It's not sodomy," Funt said.

The albino wasn't on the football team, that much was certain. There wasn't enough mass on those shoulders to support the compact sedan's worth of hard plastic the players strapped to themselves before games. Besides, it probably wasn't such a good idea for him to spend that much time in the sun, anyway.

"Funt, sucking dick is the definition of sodomy. Don't you read the Bible?"

Sodomy: any variation of sexual contact that is considered unnatural or abnormal, i.e. oral intercourse. Some boys collect stamps. Some boys memorize the naughty words in the dictionary. Different strokes. Different folks.

"Knock it off!"

"Dude, relax," the albino said.

"I am relaxed," Funt said. "I just don't want it to be awkward around you when I'm with her."

The albino opened his backpack and took out a small, blue toiletries bag. "What am I gonna say?"

He was probably just going to shave or pluck his eyebrows or something. It didn't make much sense to Dixie, but then again, neither did jockstraps.

"You don't need to say anything," Funt said. "I'll just see you and keep hearing all this evil crap in my head."

"What you should be worrying about is bringing that slut home for Sunday pot roast with your mother."

"My mom won't know she's a slut."

Funt bent down to grab something out of his sock, then stood up and handed the albino a thin roll of dollar bills. They were most likely settling some kind of fantasy-football bet. It was like an organized religion for these morons.

"Dude, she's practically got it branded on her forehead,"

the albino said. "These girls, they just have a different look in their eyes, you know?"

The albino opened the bag and took out the shaving necessaries.

Huh, that's funny; Dixie had never seen anyone shave with a hypodermic needle before . . . and no razor . . . or shaving cream. Pretty much just the needle and a few vials of liquid. It must be European.

"Say me and Nicole are out Cosmic Bowling or something," Funt said. "And you show up, and I've got my arm around her, and I'm looking at you, and I'm looking at her. . . . Dude, it's gonna be awkward."

With expert, nimble fingers, the albino uncapped the needle, plunged out the liquid from the vial, and tapped out the bubbles. "Nobody goes to the bowling alley anymore, you douche."

Dixie himself hadn't returned since a disastrous eighth birthday party. He preferred not to reflect on the details but at least learned that "weak upper-body strength" and "open-toed sandals" were a dangerous combination. On the plus side, his mom was a real quick mender.

"Just don't call her a slut is all." Funt pulled down his football shorts and leaned over the sink. It was the hairiest ass Dixie had ever seen without an attached tail.

The albino moved behind him and grabbed Funt's right butt cheek. "You're a bitch."

"I'm not a bitch."

"Then don't choose your slutty ass girlfriend over your bros."

The albino stuck the needle into a relatively clear patch of skin and injected the liquid, then pulled it out.

"Fuck you," Funt said and pulled up his shorts.

The albino rested the empty needle on the sink, and dropped the bag into his backpack. "You should thank me for being such a good friend to talk to you about this."

"Shut up."

The albino walked away. Funt splashed up some water from the faucet and then followed.

Something light clinked against the overflow of aluminum cans in the trash can.

And then, silence.

Dixie kept his feet rigid against the door until his heart slowed down. He was off schedule; the magic would have to wait until after his afternoon cartoons and fruit leather. But this was more important than bowel regularity or processed snack foods: this was news.

He dropped his feet down from the wall and breathed out deep. On second thought, maybe there was enough time for just a little bit of the magic, after all.

Chapter 3

Monday, 1:50 p.m.

After flushing, wiping, flushing, washing his hands, and flexing (those pushups were already producing dividends), Dixie turned his attention to the trash can next to the urinals.

Cans, binder paper, and what looked like a used condom tucked inside of a banana peel were stacked over the lip of the trash can, and balanced on top of the mess, the cherry on the refuse sundae: the syringe.

Dixie reached for the syringe, but then stopped himself. He returned to the toilet stall and constructed a protective mitt from a wad of toilet paper.

Ever so delicate, ever so tender, Dixie plucked the non-sticky end of the syringe out from its nest of soda cans and brought it up to his glasses for closer examination.

Yep, it's a syringe. Dixie considered sniffing it to determine the contents but decided not to chance jamming it into his nose.

He set the syringe onto the edge of the washbasin, took out his notebook, and flipped to a fresh page. He was pretty sure there was a story in all this, maybe even a front pager, but there was only one way to be absolutely certain:

"The Mel Nichols Six W Test: Who, What, When, Where, How, and Why."

Dixie shook his head and pulled his pen from the spine of the notebook; for such a brilliant man, Nichols really ought to have thought up a better title. Something like "The Mel Nichols News Blast!" or "The Mel Nichols Five W and an H Test." Sure, that last one might not look so good on a T-shirt, but at least it would accurately account for the "How."

The rest was pure genius.

To test his story, a reporter compared the known facts of the situation against the six-part rubric. If any of the factors could not be accounted for, the reporter shifted his investigation to fill in the missing information. A great story answered every question, as well as "commented on the human condition," which Dixie never really understood, but it sure did sound pretty.

Nichols's method didn't get much respect from so-called "serious" reporters and academics, but it was the foundation of Dixie's journalism career, and he didn't plan on deviating from a proven winner.

Dixie filled in the facts from the situation and compared it against the standard:

WHO: Funt. Some albino.

That part was easy. Dixie still didn't know *who* the albino was, but that should be simple enough to figure out. All he had to do was flip through the class portraits in the yearbook and look for the bright spot. That, or stake out the sunscreen aisle at the Wal-Mart. It was basic journalism, really.

WHAT: Steroids?

At least, that made the most sense for a football player, and just as soon as he figured out how to test for what was in the syringe, he'd prove it.

WHEN: Monday at 1:53 p.m.

1:53 p.m. and 38 seconds to be exact, with a special thanks to the fine folks at Swatch.

WHERE: Boy's bathroom in locker room.

Obviously, Funt valued swollen muscles and spiked aggression over adequate ventilation and pleasant decor. Oh well, Dixie supposed there was no figuring for the tastes of a junkie.

HOW: Funt bought drugs from the albino.
The albino is the dealer?

That seemed tidy enough.

WHY: To get huge. Huger?

Of course, if Dixie looked anything like Funt, he'd be a lot more concerned with *decreasing* body mass. Like, maybe shooting up some Slim-Fast, instead. Not only was it legal, but it didn't shrivel the testicles. There were a variety of benefits.

Dixie looked through the list and smiled. This was it. He finally had a chance to publish something real. He finally had a chance to write about the football team without using the words "brave" and "young" and "heroes." He finally had a chance to get back at those assholes for the years of wedgies and Russian cootchies.

This was the "scoop" he'd been waiting for. Even Ms. Trasker couldn't keep something this powerful off the front page. Well, unless the homecoming floats were particularly sparkly that year.

It still didn't pass Nichols's test. Not yet. He still had to confirm WHAT was in the syringe and HOW the albino fit into it all, but Dixie knew that he could piece all that together. He just needed to stash the syringe somewhere safe until he could figure out the next step.

But not in here.

He couldn't keep anything of value in his locker; he learned that painful lesson early on (if only the TI-89 graphing calculator could process toilet water as easily as quadratic equations. Rick pooping on top was just mean-spirited), and while the syringe was waterproof, he didn't want to chance compromising the forensic evidence.

That just left one option: his desk in the *Wildcat* office. The only other person with a key to the room was Ms.

Trasker, and unless he wrapped the syringe in cigarettes and Kit Kat bars, it would be safe.

Of course, this presented its own share of problems.

The *Wildcat* office was clear across campus, and that meant sneaking over there undetected and getting back to the gymnasium before PE was over. There were immediate penalties for missing final roll call, and Dixie didn't want to spend his lunch hour doing calisthenics in the wrestling room while Coach Hamm sweated off his morning bourbon.

He walked out of the bathroom and heard the distinctive squeak of worn leather against the wood floor of the gymnasium; the freshman girls' class must still be in the volleyball unit.

Freshman. Girls. Volleyball.

Dixie allowed the full implications of that situation to wash through his gray matter, but the cool glass pressed against his hand snapped him back to reality. Syringe. Syringe. Syringe.

He pushed open the back door, walked outside, and scanned across his field of vision. Nothing there. He put on his glasses. Much clearer. Still nothing.

Well, that took care of the first obstacle. All that left was sneaking across campus and back in the next twenty minutes. That was obstacle number two.

Stilton High School was built in the early 1930s to accommodate three hundred students with four buildings (cafeteria, library, office, and multistory classroom known as the Tower) that surrounded an open grass quad.

As the town's population swelled in the 1970s, the school was unable to accommodate the influx of students, and lacking the room for permanent expansion (the school was bordered by downtown on one side, a large hill on the other, and bisected by a creek), classroom trailers were wheeled and crammed into the available space as a temporary solution until the school board could organize the construction of a new, more adequate structure.

In the ensuing thirty years, the school board never got around to building the new campus (though they did accomplish some groundbreaking legislation on skirt length) but luckily, the town's population leveled off. And that was a good thing—the only remaining space for trailers would have been the football field, and the inevitable mob of torch-wielding football fans would have really interfered with future school board meetings.

The *Wildcat* office was in the basement of the Tower, and though the direct path from the gymnasium was relatively short, it also required walking through the quad. That was a bad idea: the school's security guards, Dale and Parksie, always posted themselves there to get the most detection from the least locomotion. Nice guys, really, but as hard and leathery as the old rodeo belts eclipsed by their sagging stomachs.

So, that meant the overland route. Which not only brought Dixie in direct view of the road, but also crossed in front of the main office. It was risky, sure, but the situation was desperate enough to warrant moving forward with the plan.

Besides, as a master of the first-person shooter video game, Dixie was well experienced in the arts of infiltration and general sneakery.

He took a low crouch and duckwalked from the protective brick facade of the gymnasium to the cover of a propane tank twenty yards to the east.

Something crinkled on the far side of the propane tank, and Dixie dropped belly first onto the ground. Mother wouldn't like the stain, but those were concerns for civilian Dixie. Military Dixie was stalking Charlie.

He army-man crawled to the edge of the fence and peered around the corner to sight his enemy.

A short, plump girl with dyed black hair and pale, caked makeup leaned against a picnic table in front of the gymnasium, smoking a cigarette. At least Dixie assumed she was plump. It was hard to figure much in the way of body shape under her PE sweatshirt, and her legs looked skinny enough, but her face was plump.

"Hey," Dixie said.

And what a beautiful face it was.

The girl flicked ash from the end of her cigarette and nodded. "Hey."

"Are you okay?' a voice asked from behind Dixie.

Dixie rolled over and looked up at the voice: Mr. Nelson. Art teacher. Ponytail. Tweed jacket. How that jacket stayed free of paint was always a mystery to Dixie, but he sure made one hell of a fine silk screen.

"I'm fine," Dixie said. "I'm . . . I just fell."

He looked back to the picnic table, but the girl was

gone. That was a real shame; their conversation had been going so well.

"You fell?"

Dixie turned back. "Yeah . . . back there . . . I got dizzy?"

Well, at least that worked for his grandmother. Of course, it also got her placed in an assisted-living facility, but that might not be so bad. Dixie already liked soft food and bocce ball.

"And that's why you're crawling on the ground?"

Rats. Dixie looked past Mr. Nelson and saw the window of his classroom, directly in the sight line of his stealth maneuver. This wasn't going on the highlight reel.

It was time for a little jazz. "Yeah, I . . . uhh . . . I must have blacked out, because . . . my head hurts."

"I see." Mr. Nelson took the break in conversation to look Dixie over. Not a good sign.

"So, have you been teaching here long, Mr. Nelson?"

"Why aren't you with your class?"

Dang. Dang. Dang.

"I uhh . . . I needed to get my medicine."

"Is that your medicine in the toilet paper, son?"

The word "medicine" floated out neon and green in the space between Dixie and Mr. Nelson.

"No."

No? Hundreds of hours spent listening to *Hannity & Colmes*, and that was the best he could come up with? Pathetic.

"Why don't you show me what's in your hand?"

"No," Dixie said. It wasn't the most elegant defense but at least had the strength of consistency behind it.

"Maybe you should come with me to the office."

Dixie dropped his eyes from Mr. Nelson, rolled to his feet, and took a few tentative steps toward freedom.

"Uhh . . . actually, that's fine. . . ." Dixie walked faster. "Thanks for taking the time to check up on me, though, it was a real kindness. . . . I guess I'll be seeing you around, then."

Mr. Nelson didn't try to stop him. That was unexpected.

He looked up from his sneakers to assess the situation: Mr. Nelson was nowhere to be seen. Check that. He was to be seen, just not in the expected location. Mr. Nelson was inside his classroom now. On the telephone.

This was bad.

A thousand plans crammed into Dixie's mind and blocked shut the birth canal of conscious decision. He didn't have a plan, just an uncontrollable impulse to pump his skinny legs and arms toward anything that was open and free and the hell away from where he was.

Dixie skidded around the corner and leaped up the stairs to the quad. Mr. Wilson, the biology teacher, once told Dixie that the only remaining human instinct was the baby's homing sensor for its mother's nipple. Apparently, Mr. Wilson never had to run away from anything before. Because if Dixie were running on anything other than animal instinct and fear, he would have done things differently:

1. He would have stashed the syringe on the roof or under a rock and retrieved it once the heat blew over.

2. He would have ducked into a convenient bathroom or bush and hid out until he could mingle into the confusion of the between-class shuffle.

3. And if he had to keep on running, he wouldn't have chosen to do so through the quad and directly in front of Dale and Parksie, flap of toilet paper trailing in his wake like a rhythmic-gymnastics prop, just in case they hadn't noticed him the first time.

But that's what he did.

Dixie didn't even know that Dale and Parksie had taken up the chase. The steady clop of cowboy boots closing in on him was impossible to hear over the loud rasp of acid pumping through his lungs.

Had Dixie known they were behind him, he wouldn't have taken an inhaler break in the dirt courtyard between the swimming pool and foreign language trailers.

Failing that, if Dixie knew that Dale used to be an especially mean and hard-hitting linebacker for this very Stilton High oh so many years and international conflicts ago, he would have braced himself for the flying body tackle coming his way.

And if Dixie knew that was going to happen, he wouldn't have chosen that exact moment to put his very breakable, very shrapnel-like inhaler next to his very soft and shrapnel-sensitive gums.

But he did all that, too.

And if Dale were to have taken full inventory of his trick shoulder, bone-on-bone knees, zippered chest, and recently plastic-enhanced hip, he might not have thrown himself at full speed into another human body and the inevitable collision with earth following soon afterward (though both were remarkably soft representatives of their kind), and especially not if he realized that this particular soft human body was holding something especially unsoft in his hand.

But that's just what Dale did.

By the time Parksie arrived (though a faster athlete than Dale during their respective playing years, he possessed even creakier knees than his partner), the scene appeared as such:

Dixie was knocked out. No surprise there.

Dale was still conscious, but suffered the worst of the collision—arm twisted at an impossible angle, knees fused together in a desperate search for cartilage, and a toilet paper–covered syringe sticking out of his neck.

On the good-news front, his surgically enhanced hip held up remarkably well to the strain, though its twin now required a similar operation.

Parksie looked down at the bodies, and allowed himself a dip of tobacco to cogitate upon the full implications of the happenings and the most appropriate course of action to follow.

"Hey, Dale, you got something sticking out your neck."

"Oh?"

The two men took a break from the conversation for spitting. Parksie, tobacco juice. Dale, blood.

"You see me tackle that peckerwood?"

Chapter 4

Monday, 2:30 p.m.

Dixie blinked back into consciousness. The ceiling was covered in gray, chipped paint. Either he was in the gulag, or the school was running behind on their maintenance budget. He wasn't sure which one he'd prefer.

The tinny vibrations of desktop-radio easy listening bounced through the walls. So, it's the gulag, then.

He sat up in the cot and felt a sharp ache in the center of his back where his flesh and bones had folded themselves over the hard metal bar. There might have been a layer of fabric sandwiched somewhere in the mix, but Dixie wasn't sure. Whoever designed Army cots obviously never slept on Army cots.

Dixie checked his surroundings: bad carpet, refrigerator, an old microwave balanced on top of a card table. This was the teacher's lounge.

He swiveled his feet onto the ground and breathed deep. All that left was making an explosive device from a sausage hot pocket and a packet of pepper flakes, and he would be well on his way to freedom. Or a satisfying midafternoon snack. In all the excitement of discovering the syringe and getting knocked unconscious, Dixie had missed lunch.

The cell door swung open, and Dixie braced himself for his daily ration of old bread and cane beating.

Instead, all he saw was a beard.

There was more to Mr. Steinberg than the facial hair, but Dixie couldn't focus on much else. The beard was a great asymmetrical beast, stretching from his cheek to Adam's apple. His mouth wasn't visible through this pelt, but Dixie assumed he took nourishment through a slit about a knuckle below the nose.

The exposed skin under Mr. Steinberg's shirtsleeves was tan and muscular, and if it weren't for the woodland animal nesting across his chin, Dixie suspected that he would be quite handsome.

"How you doin' there, buddy?" Mr. Steinberg asked, the coarse hairs around his mouth vibrating then settling like the prongs of a tuning fork.

A mathematics teacher by training, Mr. Steinberg assumed the mantle of school counselor after years of gentle suggestion and a school budget crisis rival to that of a small Caribbean nation. Mr. Steinberg wasn't a trained counselor, so he had developed a personal style of psychoanalysis that consisted almost entirely of hugging.

He told people to call him Huggy Bear, and wore a T-shirt most days that advertised the same. Freud. Jung. Huggy Bear.

"Uh . . . fine, Mr. Steinberg."

"Mr. Steinberg?" The beard whistled back and forth as he gave an exaggerated look over both shoulders. "What, is my dad in here? Call me Huggy Bear."

"Okay," Dixie said as a continuous loop of "please-don't-ask-me-to-hug-you" ran through his mind at double speed.

"Would you like a hug?"

Dixie sighed. So much for telepathic projection.

"No thanks." Dixie scooted back on the cot until his shoulders pressed against the wall. "I'm doing pretty okay over here."

The beard moved closer, and Dixie felt under the mattress for something blunt and heavy to throw at him. Nope.

"Let's see what we got here." Huggy Bear untucked a manila folder from under his arm and squinted at the paper inside. "Dixie Nig Goo Yun . . . did I get that right?"

That was actually one of the better attempts Dixie had heard in recent memory. "Uhh . . . it's kinda more like *win*, but you know, close enough."

Huggy Bear nodded and looked back at the paper. "And your parents are Dario and Linda Presto?"

"Yeah."

"Oh . . ." Huggy Bear wrinkled his forehead and closed the file. "Wait, so what . . . why is your name Nig Gun Yawn, then?"

"It's kind of a long story."

Actually, it wasn't. Like most hippies, Dixie's first adoptive father believed in fostering the individual spirit of the child, and so gave his son a unique handle: Dixon "Dixie" Nguyen (the name on his adoption papers).

Dixie appreciated the Presto family's acceptance and generosity but still decided to keep the name his first adoptive father had given him when he moved to Stilton. It was part of his identity, a reminder of his heritage, and besides, his pajamas were already monogrammed.

"I respect your right to privacy." Huggy Bear placed the folder on top of the microwave and stepped closer to the cot. "Are you sure about that hug? You've had a pretty rough day."

This all seemed strangely familiar to Dixie, but from where? Oh yeah, it was that after-school special . . . where the kid gets molested by his uncle. Wait . . .

"Yeah, I think I'll pass." Dixie reached his hand behind his back and tensed it into a claw of death.

"How am I supposed to be the Huggy Bear if I don't give any hugs?"

"I don't want a hug!"

The beard moved back, but the hairs around the mouth opening remained stuck in smile formation. Dixie suspected it took several minutes for the thing to register emotional change.

"I'm sorry, Mr. Stein . . . I mean, Mr. Huggy Bear—" Dixie started, but something louder kept him from finishing.

"Where did you get the dope, you little thug?"

It wasn't Huggy Bear's voice, but Dixie couldn't see anything beyond the beard. Maybe he kept a leprechaun in there; that would be magical.

"Where did you get it?"

A meaty hand pushed Huggy Bear out of the way, and Principal Restano's equally meaty face shot down into spray-zone proximity with Dixie's T-zone. Evidently, somebody had garlic for lunch.

"Principal Restano," Huggy Bear said. "That's not an appropriate way to address our young friend."

"Stay out of this, Steinberg!" Restano turned and drilled the tip of his finger into Dixie's chest. "I want names, punk! You kids think you can just . . ."

Restano stopped and stared at Dixie. The rage drained out of his face, and his jowls bungeed down against his neck. "Hey, aren't you on the academic decathlon team?" Restano asked.

Dixie nodded and squirmed back to take the pressure off his sternum. These weren't the ideal circumstances, but it felt good to be recognized for his efforts. Those eighth-place regional trophies don't just put themselves in the library display case.

"Oh, sorry about that. I thought you were someone else." Restano pulled his finger out of Dixie's chest and turned back to Huggy Bear. "Steinberg, why are you wasting my time with an honors student? Don't you know we have a druggie on the loose?"

Huggy Bear walked around Restano and put his hand on Dixie's shoulder. "I'm afraid this is the child in question."

"What?" Restano looked at Dixie and then back to Huggy Bear. "This kid put Dale in the hospital?"

"Huh?" That wasn't quite how Dixie remembered the

situation, but he was willing to go along with the popular opinion. His reputation could stand the boost.

Huggy Bear nodded. "I'm afraid so."

"Gosh dangit!" Restano plopped down onto a folding chair by the microwave, wiped the droplets of perspiration off his cheek flaps, and pointed at Dixie. "What the heck's the matter with you, son? You're one of the smart kids. You're supposed to be studying or volunteering at a soup kitchen or whatever, not shooting up and causing mayhem. I've already got plenty of dumb kids around here for that kinda nonsense."

"Those weren't my drugs." Dixie hated to give up the scoop on such a prime story, but he had a feeling that this whole incident would reflect poorly on his college application. "You see, I was in the bathroom, and there were these football players, and . . ."

"Be calm, young friend." Huggy Bear squeezed Dixie's shoulder. "We're gonna get you help."

Restano shook his head. "He's gonna have to get help at Big Pine with the rest of the delinquents."

For such a small town, Stilton had a remarkable amount of "troubled" young people. So many, in fact, to require opening a separate high school in the converted real estate of one of the town's many commercial failures (a combination reggae lounge and Mongolian barbecue, appropriately named "Hey Mong"). The classrooms still reeked of pork grease and bong water, but Big Pine High was up to code, and more importantly, far enough away from the regular high school to prevent any possible cross contamination.

"He's not going anywhere," Huggy Bear said.

"Come on, Ted, we have to expel him," Restano said. "We can't have students running around, hopped up on God knows what, and attacking the staff, okay? It's just bad policy."

As much as Dixie hated to admit it, Restano made a good point.

"But, Principal Restano," Huggy Bear said. "He was under the influence."

Dixie looked up at Huggy Bear. He probably wasn't referring to his asthma medication. "No, I wasn't. That's what I've been trying—"

"Exactly!" Restano pointed at Dixie. "He was high! We can't have that."

Huggy Bear sat down on the cot next to Dixie. "According to state law, no student can be expelled until they are first placed in an on-site rehabilitation program."

Restano leaned forward. "What?"

"Unless he has another drug offense within the next semester, he is to remain here and under the care of a professional counselor." Huggy Bear pointed to himself. "Until such time as said counselor deems the rehabilitation complete."

Dixie smiled; that great, glorious, bearded man. Sure, the prospect of drug counseling with Huggy Bear was terrible enough, but he'd get excused from that once he finished the story and wouldn't get stabbed by some disgruntled hick at Big Pine in the meantime. It was a nice compromise.

This might even warrant a hug later on, but Dixie was

unable to suppress the molestation anxiety long enough to cement the plan. Maybe they could shake hands. That was a good start.

Restano breathed deeply and rested his chin flaps against his chest. "So, can he still do the academic decathlon, then?"

"We'll see how his treatment goes."

Restano nodded, pushed up from his chair, and walked across to the door. He reached for the handle and stopped. "Wait, don't we need to call the cops or something?"

Dixie shot a smile at Huggy Bear, and waited to be rescued again.

"Of course," Huggy Bear said and patted Dixie on the knee. "The police should be here any minute."

And suddenly, Dixie felt the pressing need for a hug.

Chapter 5

Monday, 9:17 p.m.

Dixie's father stopped his truck at the red light next to the downtown liquor store, and turned to his wife. "You can't go on protecting that boy for the rest of his life!"

And then the silence. Sergeant Presto tended to space out his vindictiveness when he was especially angry, and though Dixie was always intimidated by the man (he imagined it had something to do with the gun collection and police uniform), tonight was the first time that he'd ever been truly terrified of his father.

Dixie understood the sergeant's frustration; having a son arrested by his colleagues/drinking buddies had to rank among his worst nightmares (right between the Raiders moving back to LA, and Dixie coming home for Thanksgiving dinner with a Puerto Rican lover named Timmy), but he had bigger things on his mind than his father's personal and professional humiliation. Like the tire iron, which was not so much on his mind as digging into his knee bone.

His parents and brother, Brandon, shared the front bench of the truck, while Dixie folded himself into the backseat/tool chest/trash can area. That part wasn't intended as punishment; it was just that nobody else in the family was quite svelte or limber enough to squeeze past the front seat.

The Prestos had stopped at Burger King for dinner but hadn't offered Dixie the option of supersizing his combo meal. Dixie assumed this *was* part of his punishment. That was okay, though—the orphan with-hardship angle worked out well enough for most everyone in Charles Dickens, and besides, french fries gave him the winds.

Dixie heard more slobbers from the hulking bookends in the front row and decided that open-mouth chewing was a hereditary trait. He supposed that his freedom from the predisposition was one of the benefits of being adopted. So, that made one.

The similarities between Brandon and the sergeant didn't end at food processing. They shared the same pants size, neck width, and fondness for the sweatier endeavors of man. Brandon was softer around the eyes, but Dixie wasn't sure if that was stray genetics from Mrs. Presto, or if the sergeant's steely, penetrating gaze manifested itself at a more advanced stage of male Presto development. Perhaps sometime after he grew out his first mustache.

"They sure as hell wouldn't hire a doper down at the station!" the sergeant bellowed.

Dixie's brother swiveled back and shrugged. Brandon knew better than to interrupt the sergeant during one of his truck monologues, but Dixie still appreciated the gesture, no matter how small.

Brandon was a senior at Stilton High and, up until this year, the starting left tackle on the football team. He'd quit the team before his final season to focus on academics and student government after learning that colleges were generally more interested in honors students and class presidents than two-hundred-pound offensive linemen with stubby arms. The world could be a confusing place, sometimes.

Dixie nodded at his brother and forced up a weak smile. Brandon was remarkably bright for somebody who'd spent the past few years repeatedly bashing his head against hard plastic.

More smacks, a deep, exploratory slurp from the sergeant's Dr Pepper, and, "I hope all this is getting through that doped up head of yours!"

Mrs. Presto responded with a snort. Dixie wasn't sure if that was a snort in his defense, against him, or strictly sinus related. It's difficult to read a snort.

"Let me finish, Linda—"

So, it was a pro-Dixie snort, after all. Thanks, Mom.

"—You keep this up, and you'll be heading straight to juvie, and a boy like you . . . well, juvie just isn't a very good place for a boy like you."

Dixie agreed. He had a hard enough time at high school, and that was without the added challenges of gangs and hepatitis.

"But, those weren't my drugs. . . ." Dixie said.

"Don't start with that locker room crap again!" The sergeant stopped yelling to give full focus to the left-hand turn. He was a careful driver in all circumstances but especially so during moments of emotional stress. "Every junkie has an excuse, son. I've heard them all."

Dixie traced a frowny face against the condensation of the back window. This wasn't going nearly so well as he had hoped.

"You're lucky I've got connections with Judge Fitch," the sergeant said. "He's agreed to do us a favor."

Dixie smiled; he always suspected there would be advantages to having a father in law enforcement. Well, besides the family day picnic. That was pretty sweet. "Awesome! So, he's gonna let me off then, right?"

The sergeant took his "ten o'clock" hand off the steering wheel, and rubbed the bridge of his nose. "No, Dixie. You were arrested for assault and drug possession. . . . That doesn't just go away."

"Oh," Dixie said. It all sounded a lot worse when his crimes were listed together like that.

"But, when you plead guilty on Monday, he's gonna let you serve your term at VisionQuest."

VisionQuest. Something about that name sounded familiar to Dixie. Oh wait, there it is now—"Isn't that some kind of a death march through the Oregon wilderness?"

"It's a rehabilitation facility, honey," Mrs. Presto said. "It'll be good for you."

Rehabilitation facility. Dixie was fairly certain that's how Pol Pot described it, too.

"Is juvie still on the table?" Sure, the gangs, forced

intimacy, and heavy denim would be tough to get used to, but it was preferable to prolonged hiking, and at least in prison nobody would make him eat a boiled pinecone. Well, unless the Aryan Brotherhood had nothing else planned for their evening's entertainment.

"Trust me, Dixie . . . the six months you'll spend at that program will change your life."

Six months of chronic blisters and improvising toilet paper from tree bark. Dixie wasn't sure where the part about this being a "favor" came into play. "Are you sure you know this judge?" Dixie asked.

"You don't know how lucky you are," the sergeant said. "It usually takes three months to get a hearing, You don't wanna know how many favors I had to call in to get this thing pushed to next Monday."

Wait, three months? That didn't sound so bad. A man could pack a lot of living into three months. Also, hitchhike to Bolivia. There were a lot of options available.

"Uhh . . . they've already assigned me rehab at the high school," Dixie said, and coughed into his shirt. "So, maybe I should just go ahead and do that."

Dixie never expected that he would be grateful to spend time with Huggy Bear, but if he absolutely had to go through drug counseling, he figured it was better to do it somewhere with indoor plumbing and a manageable malaria risk.

"You mean with Steinberg?" The sergeant shook his head and grumbled something about "goddamn" and "hippies" and "waste of tax dollars." Apparently, he was familiar with Huggy Bear's work.

"Trust me," the sergeant said. "You'll do your time at VisionQuest, get a little hair on your chest, and be back in time for summer school. It'll be like none of this ever happened."

"Can't you just tamper with some evidence or something?" Dixie asked. "Problem solved, right?"

The sergeant exhaled long and deep. "No . . . and even if I wanted to, they aren't letting me anywhere near the case. It's a conflict of interest."

"What's the conflict?" Dixie asked. "I'm innocent! Why won't you listen to me?"

"Enough!" the sergeant yelled, and the truck went silent.

"It's for the best, sweetie," Mrs. Presto said.

Dixie leaned his head against the back window and closed his eyes. Ten years of straight As and no trouble, and for what? His parents didn't believe him. They wouldn't even listen to him. They just wanted him to stay quiet, ship off to VisionQuest, and pretend like none of this embarrassment ever happened.

This was bullshit.

The truck rolled across the main street by the Victorian church and the skeletal remains of a twenty-four-hour convenience store (a victim of the fatal combination of shifting market needs and grease fire) and continued down the road toward the Presto household.

"I'm innocent," Dixie said soft and low into his chest.

"What?" his mother asked.

"Nothing."

"You'll thank us for this." Sergeant Dario Presto: a man

of few words, great meaning, and denim shirts. Not necessarily in that order.

"So how many days are you suspended from school?" Brandon asked as he caber tossed his backpack onto the top bunk.

"Uhh . . . nobody really gave me an exact number," Dixie said, and ducked onto the lower bunk. "I think they just want to keep me in the brig until the hearing."

The "brig" wasn't quite so bad as it sounded. There were no iron bars or uniforms or guards with blunt weapons and loose morals. Instead, it was a small room in the school's office where students served out the term of their suspensions doing light clerical work for the secretarial pool. The arrangement seemed much more like a slave-labor scam than any kind of punishment structure to Dixie, but he didn't mind. He actually found stapling quite relaxing.

"That's all?"

"There's also some rehab . . . some community service." Dixie curled into the fetal position on his bed. It was a good position for thinking. Also, crying. It was a versatile position.

"Oh," Brandon said. "Sucks."

"Yeah."

It took thirteen years of daily practice and strategy for Brandon to refine the ideal method of scaling the bunk bed without the indignity of using the small wooden ladder. He began by using Dixie's mattress as a foothold to spring to the adjacent dresser, then coiled and flexed into a modified Fosbury flop onto the mattress.

Dixie watched the support beams shiver and sway as his brother searched for the night's sleeping position. He needed an ally. This was much too complicated for him to handle on his own, anymore.

"Uhh . . . Brandon?"

Brandon grunted from the top bunk. "What?"

"You . . . you think I'm innocent, right?"

"Uhh . . ." Brandon coughed and fidgeted on his mattress. "That's uhh . . . you stabbed Dale with a syringe, Dixie."

"I know it doesn't look good, but I'm telling the truth about the other stuff. You believe me, right?"

The upper bed springs creaked and Brandon breathed deep. "Well . . . you're my brother and . . . I'm there for you, no matter what and all—"

Brandon's cell phone rang from beneath the pile of dirty clothes next to the bed.

"Flubb!" came from the upper bunk, in screaming-through-pillow talk, which Dixie roughly translated as the F word.

Brandon wasn't quite so swift in his dismount. He probed for Dixie's mattress with his dangling feet for a few frantic kicks before he was safely on the ground and stomping toward his phone.

"Hello?"

Dixie watched the dark outline of his brother pace around the room, and after three minutes of arguing and some expertly strung together profanity, Brandon flipped his cell phone shut and exclaimed something that would be translated as "Flubb!" if spoken through a pillow.

Brandon knocked against the wood frame of the bunk bed and ducked his head into Dixie's compartment. "There's some trouble with the homecoming float. . . . We'll finish this later, okay?"

"Sure."

Brandon grabbed his jeans off the floor and walked out the door.

And he was gone.

Dixie hugged his knees to his chest. Nobody believed him. Nobody would help him. He was alone.

That was okay, though. He could solve this on his own. He just needed to think through a creative solution:

1. Sneak into gypsy caravan. Start new life as flamenco dancer in Albania.

This one might be difficult. Gypsy caravans didn't make their way through Northern California too often, and all that garlic probably wouldn't be good for his complexion, besides.

Moving on . . .

2. Hitchhike to San Francisco. Become a street kid.

Now, that might not be so bad. He already knew the basics: buy some complicated pants, hold up a funny sign . . . provide affordable sexual relief to the city's miscellaneous perverts and violent offenders. Yuck.

No. Nope. *Nein.* Never.

Dixie squeezed his knees to his chest a little tighter. That left just one option:

3. Prove his own innocence.

It didn't matter that everyone in town thought he was a

lying junkie—no top-heavy football player was going to make him sleep on a plastic tarp with a bunch of runaways.

He could solve this on his own; he just needed to figure out what Funt was shooting up in that syringe . . . and steal another sample of his drugs . . . and stay out of jail. . . .

Damn.

Oh well, the hearing wasn't until next Monday. A week seemed like plenty of time to crack a drug conspiracy.

Dixie rolled over to face the blank spot on the wall between his Doonesbury calendar and dragon poster. He projected headlines against the uneven crags of paint:

DRUG SCANDAL AT STILTON HIGH SCHOOL, FOOTBALL SEASON CANCELED AMIDST REPORTS OF MASSIVE CORRUPTION

LOCAL SECURITY ENFORCEMENT TERRORIZED BY ASIAN YOUTH

Dixie snuggled against his pillow and smiled; this might even trump the bonfire rally.

Chapter 6

Dixie had hole punched and stapled his way through his first few hours in the "brig," before receiving his first visitor. He didn't need the distraction. The work had a certain rhythm that coincided perfectly with the easy listening in the secretarial pool next door. That Celine Dion could really belt out a tune.

"Are you trying to kill me, Dixie?"

Unfortunately, this visitor was Ms. Trasker.

"Hello, ma'am."

"Don't you hello me, you little junkie!"

The background muzak quieted as the secretaries craned their necks to take in the drama.

Ms. Trasker grabbed Dixie by the flaps of his collar and pulled him close. "A drug addict! This whole time. And I trusted you!"

Dixie stared at the veins bulging in Ms. Trasker's hands and wondered why everyone so readily believed that he was a drug addict. He didn't steal, he didn't miss deadlines, there weren't even any track marks on his arms. But you stab one security guard with a hypodermic—

Mrs. Trasker's grip on Dixie's shirt tightened. Well, so much for the elastic cling on that collar, Dixie thought; at least the drooping fabric would show off future crops of chest hair. That look seemed to work well enough for Magnum P.I.

"I'm not a drug addict, Ms. Trasker, it's—"

"So, you just like running around with needles then, huh? What was it? Steroids? Steroids, Dixie!" Ms. Trasker released Dixie's collar and hugged her arms around his head. Menopause was a confusing time for everyone involved. "Dixie, Dixie . . . you weren't doing this for the girls, were you?"

"No." Dixie twisted his face to find the air pocket in her armpit. "There were these two guys, and I'm not sure if it was steroids, but—"

"The girls are gonna like you for you, Dixie, not your big muscles and hip-hop lifestyle."

"Wait, listen, they weren't—"

Ms. Trasker crushed Dixie's cheek against her bosom. "Shh . . . shh . . . we're gonna get you help."

Dixie wanted to speak, but that would require moving his lips against Ms. Trasker's breasts—well, three layers of fabric, and then the breast, but an unpleasant prospect, regardless.

He decided to compromise by speaking slow. "The drugs weren't mine. I'm onto something big here, and—"

"Of course you are, sweetie." Ms. Trasker stroked Dixie's hair. "Of course you are . . . shh."

Dixie wriggled against her grasp. Nothing doing. For being his closest encounter with a female breast since—ever really (the orphanage had a pretty strict formula-only policy), the moment was nowhere near as sexually satisfying as Dixie anticipated. Lack of oxygen was probably a factor.

"Wouldyouletgoandlistentome!" The words escaped Dixie's mouth before he could slow the momentum of his frustration.

Ms. Trasker's forearm tightened on Dixie's windpipe and forced out a throaty squeak. "What are you talking about, Dixie?" she asked.

"Whacc yaa lacchh goh maah throaa, ahh cann breaahh!"

"Excuse me?"

The increasingly red tinge in Dixie's cheeks quickly answered her question.

"Oh!" Ms. Trasker released him. "Sorry."

Dixie rubbed his neck and searched for the inhaler in his pocket; he'd almost forgotten why he hadn't tried out for the wrestling team.

Ms. Trasker pushed aside the stack of papers and vaulted her ass onto the desk in front of Dixie. "So, what's this all about, then?"

"I know how all this looks, but I'm innocent." Dixie leaned in close. "I'm onto something big here. I saw a football player taking drugs and—"

"And some campus celebrity's really the guilty one, and you're just a victim of circumstance, right?"

Dixie hesitated; he had no idea that Trasker had such refined powers of deduction. She must be sober. "Uhh, yeah, that's pretty much it exactly."

"Disappointing." Ms. Trasker's face soured, and she hopped off the desk. "That's paparazzi, Dixie, totally amateur. I thought you were better than that."

"No, this really happened."

Ms. Trasker snorted and started to walk toward the door, but Dixie grabbed for the elastic waistband of her pants. The brig was nice and all, but he couldn't waste any more time with hole punching and easy listening. Not when there was a drug scandal to uncover and just six days left to prove his innocence. He had to get out of there, and as unpleasant as the prospect seemed, Ms. Trasker was his ticket to freedom.

"Don't go!" Dixie said. "I need your help."

She looked down at Dixie's hand. "That's dangerously close to sexual harassment, bucko."

"I can prove I'm innocent," Dixie said. "Just help me get out of here . . . I'll do anything you want."

Ms. Trasker narrowed her eyes as the wheels of her brain labored and clicked. "Anything?"

Besides sex. Anything but sex. No sex. Not with you. Maybe a kiss, but definitely nothing in the way of penetration.

"Yes." Dixie tried to gulp, but couldn't summon the necessary lubrication. "Anything."

Ms. Trasker nodded and then slapped Dixie's hand off her pants. "First of all, stop talking about whatever jack-assery you've got planned, okay? You're probably going to get arrested again, and I don't want to be a knowing accomplice."

Dixie nodded. It took a lot for a teacher at Stilton High School to get fired, but that was probably just enough to get the job done. "Check."

"Second, you will finish reporting on homecoming, and I mean everything."

"Down to the last sequin."

"I'm serious, Dixie. You better be at the bonfire rally tonight."

"You got it."

She reached down and smoothed the disturbed fabric on her pants. "Third, you will continue to send me articles when you get sent to prison."

Dixie took a moment to think through how many cigarettes and back rubs it would take to trade for a typewriter in the joint. It was an unpleasant thought.

"It's more like a rehab facility, and it's not even for certain that I'm going—"

"Whatever, just make sure it gets done."

It was an impossible request. Even if he found enough charcoal and trained falcons to get his articles sent out of the wilderness, he doubted that he'd have much time for writing with all the goddamn hiking and character building.

Dixie nodded. "Deal."

Of course, she could only kill him if she caught him, and

Dixie figured that by then he'd know how to blend into the forest and make a shiv out of a pinecone and the rest of that nature stuff. That ought to even the odds a bit.

"Good." Ms. Trasker clapped Dixie on the shoulder. "You better get to work, then."

"But how am I supposed to get out of here?"

"Don't worry about that." Ms. Trasker smiled. "Principal Restano still owes me a couple of favors."

Dixie didn't know what she meant by "favors" exactly, but there were rumors, and he had encountered her door unexpectedly locked during the lunch hour often enough to believe they were at least partially true.

"You think he'll let me out of here?" Dixie asked.

"Sure, and if anyone bothers you, just tell 'em you're on assignment."

Translation: as long as he held a camera, Dixie was free to wander these halls with impunity.

Dixie looked at Ms. Trasker, and she looked right back until the moment disintegrated into awkward silence. It wasn't so bad. Most of his interactions with people ended like that.

"There's one more thing, Dixie."

Dixie sighed; so, she wanted sex, after all. Oh well, he supposed that anything was better than spending prolonged periods of time in hiking boots. "Yeah?"

"I'm lonely, Dixie."

"Uh-huh." Dixie gulped hard. He didn't like where this was headed.

"I'm chaperoning the homecoming dance, and a lonely

woman shouldn't be alone at something like that, at least not with her coworkers. It's hormonal. They'll explain this to you in health class. Anyway, I need someone with me to make sure I don't make any mistakes. Do you understand?"

"No," Dixie said, and edged back in his seat.

She didn't want sex. It was something far more horrible than that.

Ms. Trasker pulled a measuring tape out of her purse and stepped toward Dixie. "You're gonna take me to the homecoming dance."

Chapter 7

Tuesday, 10:29 a.m.

Thirty minutes after Ms. Trasker finished measuring Dixie for his tuxedo and left for Restano's office, one of the secretaries informed Dixie that he had been released from in-house suspension to work on the school paper. Evidently, Ms. Trasker's meeting with Restano went well, and Dixie made a mental note to give her a congratulatory high five just as soon as he procured some industrial-strength disinfectant and latex gloves.

Unfortunately, Dixie wasn't yet exempt from all forms of punishment, and still had to deliver the city's newspaper, *The Stilton Gazette*, to the classrooms before he was officially free. It wasn't part of the arrangement he and Ms. Trasker had made, but she had already bent over backward for him (and, in all likelihood, Restano as well), and Dixie didn't want to make a fuss.

Besides, delivering the newspapers wasn't such an inconvenience, anyway; only one teacher at Stilton High utilized the resource as an integral part of his daily lesson plan. Well, the only part, really.

Mr. Sportoletti taught remedial government, and the sum lesson plan for each day consisted of two minutes of roll call, followed by free reading the newspaper until the bell rang. It was a travesty, and unfair to the students, but luckily, all involved parties (students, parents, and administration included) were just apathetic enough themselves to make the arrangement work.

Dixie opened the classroom door and paused in the threshold. "Where do you want the papers, Mr. Sportoletti?"

Mr. Sportoletti looked at him over the ridge of the newspaper (Yesterday's edition. The Jumble must have been particularly devious.) and then returned to ignoring him. Dixie assumed this meant "one on each desk, young man."

Dixie nodded ("sure thing, sir" in the man's preferred language) and started distributing.

Under normal circumstances, Dixie would have never put himself within grasping range of anyone who appeared as predisposed to violence as the students in this class. And he was careful to keep his testicles angled away from any possible sneak attacks. He did the same while waiting in line for cookies after church. Paranoid, maybe, but Dixie figured a man that didn't protect his genitals at all times didn't really deserve to have them.

He looked down at headlines in the brief interim between the slap of the paper on a desk and his shuffle to the next customer:

SCHOOL BOARD MEETS

Slap.

COUNTY FAIR

Slap.

GOVERNOR'S APPROVAL

Slap.

ANOTHER OVERDOSE

Slap.

ANOTHER OVERDOSE DEATH

Slap.

ANOTHER OVERDOSE DEATH FOUND IN WOODS

Slap.

Dixie paused at the desk and skimmed the article. "Cause of death is believed to be methamphetamine overdose."

"What?" a voice asked.

For being such an expert reader, Dixie felt that he really should have progressed beyond sounding out each word. This was starting to get embarrassing.

He looked down in the direction of the voice: it was the pretty, goth girl from outside the gymnasium. She held a black Magic Marker, and a flaming skull was drawn across her thigh in fresh ink.

"Uhh . . . hey," Dixie said, and nodded at her thigh. "Killer tat."

The goth girl grunted and dropped her gaze to outline a spiderweb on the back of her hand.

He stared at the thick, wet lines across her skin and smiled. He never imagined something like that could look so delicate and refined. The quality of the canvas was probably a factor.

Dixie momentarily considered showing her the dragon that he had been sketching across his bicep during quiet moments in the brig, but decided against it. He had just uncovered a major lead in his investigation, and besides, he really needed to finish shading the wings and tone up with some Pilates before it would be ready for public display.

He finished delivering the newspapers at double speed, then walked to the back of the room and took down a copy of the encyclopedia.

METALLURGY . . . METAZOA . . . METCHNIKOFF . . . METEOSAT . . . METHAMPHETAMINE. Bingo. Dixie skimmed through the entry:

"Synthetically produced stimulant. Manufactured from a variety of household items such as cold medicine and ammonia. Referred to as meth, speed, crank, white pony. Typically smoked, snorted, or 'bumped' (injected through syringe). Common side effects: euphoria, increased alertness and physical activity, irritability, aggression, acne, and heavy sweating."

The symptoms all seemed so familiar to Dixie, but from where? Professional wrestling? Family reunions? McDonalds? No, not that. Something closer. Something recent.

"Holy crow." The realization hit Dixie like a wet towel: it was Funt. He was violent. His skin was terrible. Dixie couldn't remember the last time he hadn't see him covered in sweat. Funt's breasts were still a bit of a mystery, but that was probably just another side effect from the meth. Or bad genetics; Dixie could go either way.

Dixie took out his notebook and flipped to the "Six W" page. This changed a few things:

WHAT: ~~Steroids~~? Meth?

Now that he thought about it, Funt looked flabby for a guy on steroids. Plus, he certainly had what Dixie imagined was the halitosis of the stereotypical junkie.

WHY: ~~Get huge. Huger~~? Boost athletic
performance through meth psychosis.

Dixie had never heard of that before, but it seemed to make sense. It probably made all that business of bashing their heads together and rolling around in the dirt much more palatable, and at least this stuff wouldn't destroy the testicles. Teeth and skin, sure, but who cared about all that sissy stuff when a guy had a perfectly healthy set of balls?

He closed his notebook and smiled; it was definitely meth. He was glad, too. Sure, it might mean a little more work in the short term, but the jocks-and-steroids angle was played out, anyway. But meth? That was fresh. That was exciting. This might even crack the national headlines if no celebrity was adopting a war orphan that week.

"Eureka!"

The entire class dropped their newspapers and turned to Dixie.

Whoops. Dixie made a mental note to keep future internal celebrations a bit more internal, or at the very least, not directly ripped off from Archimedes.

"Sorry," Dixie said. But before he took his graceful exit, he grabbed a newspaper off the desk of a comatose student in the back row. He had some research to do.

Chapter 8

Tuesday, 10:56 a.m.

It didn't take long for Dixie's investigation to get interesting.

He walked out of Sportoletti's classroom and turned down the perimeter of the quad—passing through the thick fog of stale urine that seeped out from the open door of the boy's bathroom—and onward to a relaxing afternoon of Internet research and Chex Mix in the *Wildcat* office—

"Come here!"

—At least that's what he intended to do, but the arm of the letterman jacket that snaked out of the bathroom door had different plans.

Yep, Dixie thought as the other hand reached up to muffle his screams, this was definitely an interesting start to his investigation.

"Shut up, queer!"

And it was amazing how often "interesting" and "bad" were the same thing.

* * *

Despite its convenient central location, and his frequent need for urination, Dixie had never ventured inside the quad bathroom. Actually, he'd never seen anyone go in there, which made the pervasive stink of the place a bit of a mystery.

The jock dragged Dixie across the bathroom, grabbed him by the ankles, and dangled his head over a toilet.

His glasses fell off his face, but the plastic cord that connected the stems caught against his neck before they fell into the water. The cord was a fashion liability and chafed his skin during the more humid months, but Dixie always knew it would come in handy if he just waited long enough.

Dixie stared down at the heterogeneous solution of gray water and toilet paper in the bowl and tried to seal off the bile rising (or dropping, considering the inverted gravity) in his throat. On the good-news side, the nausea distracted him from the terror. He appreciated that.

He looked up at his captor: chubby fingers, athletic shorts, a shapely pair of C-cups.

"Hey, Funt." Dixie said.

"Shut up!"

Judging by the square footage and the height of the toilet, Dixie guessed that they were in a handicapped stall. He hoped that they weren't preventing any of the intended consumers from using the facility; things were difficult enough for them, already.

More shoes squeaked across the bathroom floor. "How's it hanging, pixie dick?"

Dixie cringed; he knew that voice.

Two meaty calves and faded cross trainers walked into

the stall. "Get it? 'How's it hanging?' Come on, laugh, Tits, this is good material."

That was Rick.

Funt obeyed and Dixie's head bounced against the rim of the toilet with each heave of the jock's guts.

"Altitude!" Dixie shouted up between the crashes. "Check your altitude!"

"Shut up!" Funt said, and knocked Dixie's head against the edge of the porcelain.

"Ow!"

"Don't hurt him too much, Funt," Rick said. "Me and pixie dick still got some unfinished business."

So, Rick was the mastermind behind the kidnapping. Dixie supposed that made sense—Funt didn't seem nearly ambitious enough to plan such a mediocre felony.

"Hey, Rick," Dixie said.

Rick bent down and frowned. Or smiled. Dixie was still having some difficulty adjusting to being upside down. "You don't wanna be talking right now."

"Why?" Dixie asked, but Rick's wink and his head's rapid descent into the toilet bowl answered that question soon enough. "Oh crap—" He braced his hands against the rim of the toilet but wasn't quite strong enough to prevent the inevitable.

"Let's try this again," Rick said after Dixie's head was lifted out of the water. "Are you gonna talk?"

Dixie shook his head. Droplets of water shot off his hair and sprayed across Rick's sandals. It wasn't much for revenge but made him feel a little better, all the same.

"You shouldn't have messed with Dale." Rick shook the drops of toilet sludge off his feet and smiled. "Things are gonna start getting bad for you around here."

Wait, things were gonna *start* getting bad for him? Dixie couldn't see how it could possibly get any worse than the present. Maybe something with trained cougars or bear mace. That sounded about right.

"So if I were you, I'd stay away." Rick curled up his lips and showed fangs. "Just leave, faggot. Nobody wants you here."

As much as Dixie agreed in principle with Rick's request, he couldn't leave just yet. Not until he published this article and destroyed the football team with scandal. Also, he still had a few books checked out from the library.

"No." Dixie took a deep breath, stared into Rick's eyes, and held his gaze until his hair hit the water. Dramatic effect was one thing; e-coli bacteria in the eyeball, a different matter entirely.

His head was lifted back out of the water, and Dixie noticed a pair of skinny, neon-white legs standing next to Rick. The albino had arrived.

So, the gang's all here. That's good; Dixie wanted all of them to hear this. Rick didn't have the decency to declare war before attacking, but Dixie still believed in a little common civility.

"I know what!—"

Splash.

"What Funt's—"

Splash.

"Funt's doing!—"

Splash.

"Tell everyone!—"

Splash . . . and hold.

And hold.

Dixie wasn't sure how long he stayed underwater, but it was more than enough time to decide against a career in pearl diving.

He felt four more hands grab on to his legs, and after a short struggle, bring him up over the surface of the water and rest his head on the toilet seat.

"What the hell's the matter with you, Funt?" the albino shouted. "You trying to kill that kid?"

Dixie spit out the accumulated toilet water and offered a quick prayer to the gods of sanitation. He wasn't sure how a person contracted leprosy, but this couldn't be far from it.

"That little bitch was talking about me!" Funt said.

"Jesus Christ, Tits, relax!" The albino lowered his face next to Dixie's. He smelled like ripe hippie and licorice. "Care to continue?"

Dixie took a deep breath and smiled. Maybe it wasn't the swiftest move to outline his strategic advantage to his enemies, but he needed the leverage just then. Besides, it was going to be fun to watch them squirm.

"I was in the bathroom yesterday, and I know what Funt's doing!" Dixie swiveled his head around to address each of his tormentors. "And I'm not gonna stop until everyone knows about it!"

They didn't react quite like he expected.

The albino's face quickly shifted from anger to confusion to amusement. "Okay." He shuffled over to Rick, and Dixie heard the low scratching of whispers and muffled laughter.

Muffled laughter? Wait, that didn't seem right. It must be some kind of side effect from the panic.

"Guys, what are you talking about?" Funt asked.

Rick lowered his face down next to Dixie's and smiled. "That ain't no secret." He looked up at Funt and winked. "I've been hitting that since seventh grade."

Dixie tilted his head from side to side to shake free any excess water from his ear canal. He couldn't have heard that last part right.

"Yeah, I hit that, too," the albino forced out through chokes of laughter. "We all hit that."

"We all hit what?" Funt asked.

"Oh, you know, you chubby sinner." The albino shuffled his starchy legs over to Funt, and Dixie heard more low whispers.

"Hey!" Funt screamed and lifted Dixie's head up six inches. "Shut up about that!"

"All of you guys?" Dixie asked. "Really?"

Rick smiled and flicked Dixie on the forehead. "Hey, it's just one of the perks of being on the football team."

Wait, the whole football team was on meth? That meant conspiracy. Massive conspiracy. Cheating. Felonies. Maybe even some official involvement, if Dixie was lucky.

"Shut up!" Funt roared and lifted Dixie up to his belt buckle.

This was huge: the biggest scandal in the history of high-school athletics, and he had the inside track on the scoop. Well, provided he didn't get drowned in this toilet bowl first.

"Calm down, you big woman," the albino said.

Dixie looked up at Funt and cycled through his escape options:

1. Bash the back of his head into Funt's testicles. Run away in the confusion.

Yep, that was about it. And unless somebody left a spare taser gun or Ginsu knife behind the toilet bowl, this was his only chance for escape.

"Yo, Funt, you should let the dork get a piece of that, too," the albino said. "Might loosen him up."

Dixie tucked his head forward and clenched his teeth, preparing for the impact. But before he could put option one into action, a new avenue for escape became available:

2. Funt drops Dixie to attack the albino. Run away in the confusion.

It was a real shame that Dixie hadn't considered that possibility earlier—

"That's it, godammit!" Funt roared.

—Because that's exactly what happened.

"Oh fu—" Dixie started, but immediately wished that he hadn't chosen such an open mouth–dependent profanity.

In the next few seconds, Dixie learned there that there were certain advantages to being dropped headfirst into a toilet. For example:

1. The water resistance slowed his momentum just enough that he didn't crush his spinal column against the bottom of the fixture.

2. Uhh . . . actually, that was about it.

Dixie's body tilted back over the fulcrum of the toilet seat, dislodging his head from the bowl, and dropping him ass first onto the slick tiles below. He was sure it would have hurt a lot more, if he weren't so grateful just to be alive.

He looked back: Rick stood in the entrance of the stall and restrained Funt from charging through and ripping off the albino's face.

"Don't talk about her like that, you pale dickhead."

"Christ, Funt, relax," the albino said and crouched down behind the protective screen of Rick's body. "It's just a joke."

Evidently the conversation had transitioned to Funt's girlfriend while Dixie's head was stuck in the toilet. That's good; they would be distracted long enough for him to escape.

Now, that just left the escaping bit. Dixie scanned his immediate area and sighed; this was going to be difficult. He couldn't force his way past the wall of jock at the stall's entrance unless he was riding an ostrich or swinging a sock full of quarters (preferably both), and the sides of the stall were too slick with condensation and mold to climb over. Dixie stared at the glint of sunshine in the gap between the bottom of the stall and the bathroom floor. Bingo.

He lowered himself onto his stomach. There was about a foot of clearance between the floor and the stall, and with enough grunting and lubrication from the mold, Dixie squirted out into the main thoroughfare of the bathroom.

"Calm down, Funt! Just chill!"

Dixie crawled across the length of the bathroom and pulled himself to his feet against a urinal.

"Ow! Let go of me, you pussy!"

He looked back at the handicapped stall: Funt had slipped an arm past Rick's body block and latched on to the albino's earlobe.

Dixie turned to the fresh air and sunshine, then sprinted to freedom.

He zigzagged through the quad, leaped down the stairs to the cafeteria, and dove into the bed of ivy that infested the sides of the stairwell.

Dixie rolled onto his back and shot back a long, bitter spray from his inhaler. This seemed like a fine enough place to halt his retreat. He was hidden from the quad, only mildly allergic to the ivy, and if he didn't give his lungs a rest soon, they were going to explode.

He pulled an "emergency" antibacterial wipe out of his wallet, ripped open the package, and dabbed it around the more germ-sensitive areas of his face. Dixie would have preferred a session with his favorite pumice stone and an industrial-size bottle of Purel, but there was no time for that now. Not when he was sitting on the scoop of a lifetime.

Dixie took out his notebook and flipped to the "Six W" page. Quite a bit had happened in the last ten minutes, and his notes needed an update:

WHO: ~~Funt.~~ The entire football team.

Wow. Dixie stared at the entry for a few seconds. He

wondered if Woodward and Bernstein had felt something like this. It was nice.

> HOW: ~~Funt~~ The football team bought
> ~~steroids~~ meth from the albino. The albino
> is the dealer?

That just didn't feel right, though. Not anymore. How could the albino possibly have the means or connections to fuel the addictions of several dozen growing psychopaths? No, that's impossible; the albino didn't even have enough ambition to buy shoes with laces. He was just a cog in the machine, a minor player, and Dixie wouldn't have his story until he tracked down the person who was really in charge.

Let's try this again:

> HOW: ~~Funt~~ The football team bought
> ~~steroids~~ meth from ~~the albino~~ meth
> kingpin? ~~The albino~~ The meth kingpin is
> the dealer?

There, that looks better. All that left was infiltrating the county's hierarchy of meth production and distribution, and he'd have his man.

He scanned through the rest of his notes. There were still holes. Sizable holes. He still didn't know for sure WHY they were taking the meth, WHEN they started, and didn't even have a usable sample of WHAT they were taking to prove it was meth in the first place. It didn't pass Nichols's test, not even close, but at least Dixie knew WHO they were now: the privileged, popular, and worshipped. The smug assholes who had tormented him every day since kindergarten. The Stilton High football team.

And he was gonna make them pay.

Dixie closed his notebook and stared at the classroom trailer across from the cafeteria—leadership class was in session.

But he couldn't do it alone.

He stood up and walked out of the ivy, past the picnic tables, and across the splotch of grass to the leadership trailer.

It was time to see just how serious Brandon was about that unconditional love and support, after all.

Chapter 9

Tuesday, 11:07 a.m.

While most high schools were known for their athletic or academic success, Stilton High was famous for its marching band and student government. There was a two-month waiting list to try out for advanced band, and the remaining periods of general instruction were so packed that Mr. Latch, the music teacher, only learned the names of those students with extraordinary musical talent, big tits, or the potential to mature into either.

Student government was not nearly so competitive. Most students found an eventual need for the extra units to even out a failing mark or substitute for a particularly unappealing class, and since student government required nothing more than attendance and painting the occasional poster for a passing grade, it quickly became the most popular selection.

Brandon took the class for different reasons. He was the senior class president, the most powerful, respected, and feared person at the school. Or at least he got first dibs on locker selection. It sounded like a pretty sweet deal.

Dixie stopped in front of the student government trailer and sponged the remaining toilet water off his face with the back of his hand. He'd hate to besmirch his brother's political legacy with a shabby appearance.

He pulled open the door and stepped inside. Brandon stood in front of three semicircles of desks. Behind him, Fred Flintstone's face was traced in chalk on the blackboard with ME SENIOR written underneath. The theme for this year's homecoming was stupid cartoons from the 70s. As opposed to last year's theme: stupid Disney movies from the 70s. Dixie was starting to notice a trend.

"We decided on that?" Brandon paced in front of the classroom, eyes red, face pale, soul deflated. "When did we decide that?"

"Last week, you moron!" From somewhere in the second row. Dixie couldn't make out who it was exactly through the ridge of ponytails and teeth in the first two rows, but it was definitely female. "Weren't you paying attention?"

The back row was filled with an assortment of stoners and hicks, carving penises into their desks or catching a nap.

"I didn't think that was definite," Brandon said.

The ponytails in the first two rows of the firing lines nodded forward. They must be reloading for their next volley. The overwhelming hatred of the girls was surprising to Dixie; he'd always heard that women were instinctively drawn to a man in power.

"Well, it's definite!" from one of the girls. "We can't change the design now!"

He had been misinformed.

So, that just left financial success and Latin dance as the only ways Dixie could hope to attract the fairer sex. That was a shame; journalism wasn't a "high money" profession, and his progress with the *Idiot's Guide to the Lambada* hadn't been going nearly so well as he had hoped. Dixie suspected that he needed tighter pants.

"Now, let's just take a second and really think through this thing." Brandon shuffled back and forth in front of the blackboard; it was much harder to hit a moving target. "Me Senior has some pop, nobody's denying that, but the Flintstones spoke modern English, you see, and—"

"The Flintstones were cavemen!"

Brandon nodded. "Good point . . . good point . . . but, they didn't talk like cavemen, did they? I mean, I guess if we were Tarzan or something, sure, but—"

"They're cavemen!" A third voice. Dixie had a hard time distinguishing the individuals with their uniformity of dress, voice, and venom projection.

"Excuse me." Dixie hated to interrupt a conversation, even a semantic argument about Hanna-Barbera, but this was more important than social niceties. "Brandon?"

"Dixie?"

Besides, if he didn't get him out of there soon, Brandon was going to get lynched, and Dixie couldn't let that happen. Not yet. Brandon was still much too valuable to the investigation.

"Do you think I could talk to you for a second?" Dixie dropped his eyes from the harpies' gaze before they turned him to stone. "Privately?"

"Uhh . . . sure." Brandon walked around the rows of desks and turned back to the class. "Talk about the skit or something. I'll be back in five."

A large girl with too much body glitter and not enough neck stood up from the front row. "You can't leave now! The T-shirt design's due in half an hour!"

Dixie recognized her as Julie from her frequent appearances as the lead photo on the *Wildcat*'s sport page (softball, volleyball, soccer, anything that involved smashing balls, really) and frequent, verbally abusive confrontations with his brother in the parking lot.

"Five minutes." Brandon pulled Dixie outside, and shut the door. "What's the matter, Dixie?"

"Uhh . . . remember when you said you were there for me no matter what and all that? You meant that, right?"

Brandon leaned in close to Dixie and sniffed. "Why's your hair wet?"

"I went into a toilet. That's not really the issue here."

Brandon rubbed the bridge of his nose and shook his head. "Jesus Christ, Dixie. What'd you do that for?"

"It wasn't exactly a free-will kinda situation," Dixie said. "There were these football players, you see, and funny we should get on the subject, but . . ."

Dixie stopped and looked at his brother: jaw clenched, face red, neck veins tense and flaring. All that was missing was a mustache and some acne scars, and he'd look just like the sergeant.

"Who did this?"

The sergeant about to punch through a wall, that is.

Presto men didn't hide their rage well. That or process lactose.

"So, you'll help?"

"Yeah . . . just tell me who did this, and I'll whip their ass!"

Dixie smiled; he didn't think he was capable of eliciting this much anger from his brother unless it was directed at him. It was actually kinda flattering.

"Thanks. That's a sweet gesture and all, but it might be a little too high profile."

"What?" The splotches of red faded to pink on Brandon's cheeks.

"Look, here's what's going on." Dixie looked back over his shoulders to check for covert surveillance. "The football team's taking meth, maybe so they play better, I'm not really sure yet, but that's what Funt was shooting up. . . . I thought it was steroids before, but then I got kidnapped by Rick and some albino, and now I know what's really going on, and we've gotta tell the world. Did you get all that?"

Dixie looked at his brother; the crimson rage had turned to a pale white. He must still be in shock. This was some pretty mind-blowing information.

"So, here's where you come in: I'm too high profile to tail the team anymore, not after the Dale thing, plus I'm pretty sure they've got a vendetta against me, but let's not get stuck on the details. Anyway, I'm gonna need you to go undercover on the football team and get some information, like, you know, where they get the drugs, who's their supplier, all that kinda stuff. Some samples and photos or whatever would be nice, too, but you know, just do your best."

Dixie waited for his brother to grunt or nod or give him a high five, any sign of comprehension would do. Nope. He was still just staring, chalky and confused.

"Look, I know I'm asking a lot here, like you're gonna have to miss some school, and there's probably gonna be some hazing or loyalty tests or whatever before they let you into the inner circle, I'm not exactly sure how all that works, but I really need you here, man. . . . Dad's trying to send me into the forest."

Still nothing. Maybe he'd prefer a variety of options.

"Or, if you didn't want to do the whole undercover thing, I guess we could just grab one of the smaller football players and beat the information out of him. I mean, it's not really 'standard journalism' or whatever, but I'm flexible. Cool?"

Brandon reached up to squeeze the bridge of his nose, and blinked in long, pained intervals. "How high are you right now, Dixie?"

"What? No, it's the football players that are on drugs," Dixie said. "Maybe you didn't hear me right the first time—"

Before Dixie could run through his explanation again, the door opened, and Julie forced her jowls and fangs outside.

"Five minutes are up, Brandon! We need you now!" Julie slammed the door behind a cloud of face glitter.

Brandon looked at Dixie, and then back to the classroom door. "Just find someplace to lie down or drink some water or something, okay?" Brandon opened the door, and a

77

wave of bad vibes and Herbal Essence floated past into the outside air. "Don't—just don't do anything, okay? Jesus . . ."

And then he was gone.

Dixie stared at the closed door and felt a scream building up through his chest. Brandon never really believed him. He was just like his parents. He was just like everybody else. All he cared about was goddam homecoming and himself.

That prick.

Dixie turned to walk back to the office and noticed a spirit poster taped to the classroom.

NIGHT RALLY! TUESDAY 8PM! GET HOT WITH THE WILDCATS!

He stared at the poster and smiled. Brandon could keep his rude women and homecoming floats. Dixie didn't need his help. He'd finish this story on his own. Sure, Rick might drown him in the toilet or break his legs before the week was over, but that didn't matter. He was going to prove that he wasn't a lying junkie, and he knew just where to start.

Dixie ripped the poster off the wall and patted it against the lingering toilet sludge in his hair. The football team would be at the rally tonight, and his press pass would get him close enough to observe their movements and get photographic evidence of any illegal activity.

He dropped the wet paper into the trash and walked across the quad to the office. It was probably for the best that Brandon didn't help, anyway. That would mean sharing creative control of the story, and that always ended with hurt feelings and lawsuits.

Chapter 10

Tuesday, 1:30 p.m.

Despite Huggy Bear's numerous requests to the school board, limited classroom space prevented him from creating an ideal healing environment for his counseling sessions. Upon his reclassification from algebra teacher to counselor, he was assigned half of basketball-coaching legend Coach Wyatt's office. However, only three days into the partnership, Coach Wyatt threatened retirement, citing the impossibility of concentration with all the whimpering coming from the other side of the room (mostly from Huggy Bear) as well as an allergic reaction to incense.

After similar failures with the computer lab, the library, and an especially tense month in the maintenance department shed, Huggy Bear finally found a home.

As all standard physical education classes ended at fourth period, and varsity practice did not begin until sixth, the weight room was Huggy Bear's sole domain for a full fifty-minute stretch after lunch. Though not an ideal solution for either party (or permanent, as assured by the school board) a peaceful equilibrium was soon reached, as the introduction of Huggy Bear's East Indian scents greatly improved the smell of the inadequately ventilated trailer, and the athlete's motivational posters on the wall quickly became an invaluable teaching aid for Huggy Bear when encountering chronic negative thinking with his "healing partners."

Dixie was painfully familiar with the location of the weight lifting trailer, but the higher-ups at the school insisted that Parksie escort him to his counseling session.

Surprisingly, Parksie didn't hold a grudge for the Dale incident. That was nice; Dixie expected some manner of prison yard retaliation as soon as they left the watchful eyes of the front office, but Parksie didn't mind all that. In fact, chasing after Dixie's "skinny, junked-up ass" was the most fun he'd had at work since the day that streaker took a header down the cafeteria stairs.

"So, is Dale okay?" Dixie asked when they reached the weight lifting trailer.

"Sure." Parksie leaned against the metal rail of the handicapped access ramp. "That lazy sonofabitch loves the coddling."

"Will you tell him I'm sorry?"

"You can tell him yourself," Parksie said. "You know that, right?"

"I don't know." Dixie walked up the ramp and stopped in front of the door. "I'm kinda busy." He decided it was best to leave out the detail about being physically terrified of a senior citizen in traction.

"I'll pass it along. Now, go get yourself off the junk." Parksie clapped Dixie on the shoulder and ambled off to find some shade.

Dixie stood in front of the door, and a stream of cinnamon-hibiscus scent blew past his face. It was a definite improvement over the room's usual sweat-grease-nut sack aroma.

Inside, Huggy Bear was busy converting the corner next to the squatting sled into a healing space. Evidently, beanbags factored pretty heavily in the process.

"Hi," Dixie said.

"Buddy!" Huggy Bear stood up. "Come on in!"

Dixie hesitated. Big mistake. The great friendly beard skimmed across the bulk-rate carpet with long, marathoner strides. Arms wide, eyes wider. The horror.

Of the great many options available to Dixie at the moment, all involved some form of movement. For example, movement out of doorway, followed by movement to Cuba. Or, movement to free-weight stand, followed by movement of blunt object to Huggy Bear's knee, and then movement to Cuba. Unfortunately, the only movement Dixie could muster was a little quiver of the lower lip before Huggy Bear enveloped him.

But the hug wasn't as bad as Dixie expected: good pressure, comfortable distance between genitals, minimal facial hair scratchiness.

"There, there . . . you're safe now . . . Huggy Bear's got you."

Dixie responded with a few light taps on Huggy Bear's shoulder.

Huggy Bear released his grasp and pointed at the bean-bags. "Have a seat, young friend." Dixie chose the red one. That was a good, manly color.

Huggy Bear took a moment to light the remaining candles, turn off the overhead halogens, and click on a small boom box before sitting down. The music was somewhere between Bangladesh elevator and John Tesh. Not bad stuff. Dixie had to hand it to those East Indians—they really knew how to set a mood.

He looked past Huggy Bear to a poster next to the butterfly press. A man in flowing robes and a beard played soccer with a group of ethnically diverse schoolchildren. JESUS IS MY TEAMMATE curved across the top in white, fluffy cloud letters. Dixie assumed that violated some fundamental federal laws, but he didn't want to make a fuss.

Huggy Bear smiled at Dixie . . . and smiled. "Have you ever meditated before, Dixie?"

"Uhh . . . no. Not officially."

"Would you like to try?"

"No," Dixie said. "That's okay."

"Are you sure? It's a really good way to get into the healing mindset."

Also, molested. No dice, Huggy Bear. This cowboy was saving himself for marriage, or someone with questionable standards and low self-esteem. Whatever came along first, really.

"Yeah." Dixie scratched the back of his neck. "I did some yoga on my lunch break. I'm good."

"Okay," Huggy Bear said.

Well, that was easy. Dixie considered giving "I would like to leave now and get a corn dog" a shot. Huggy Bear didn't seem like the confrontational type.

"Who's the new guy?"

The hairs around Huggy Bear's mouth tilted up to right angles. "Welcome, Brynn!"

Dixie turned toward the voice and smiled. It was the goth girl. He'd been hoping for another chance at conversation. He would have preferred slightly different circumstances, a candlelight dinner in Paris, or the bathtub at a Super 8 motel, perhaps, but he was willing to compromise.

The girl stared at Dixie. "Who are you?"

"Brynn, I would like you to meet our new healing partner, Dixie," Huggy Bear said. "Dixie, this is Brynn."

"What, he doesn't talk?" Brynn walked inside and stood over Dixie. "Is he retarded or something?"

Huggy Bear's mouth hairs tilted down several degrees. "No, Brynn. He's just shy, and you know that we don't use negative language in this environment."

Shy. He liked the sound of that. Johnny Depp was shy, and he seemed to do okay with the ladies.

Brynn plopped down onto the beanbag next to Dixie's, and a cloud of trapped air whooshed up into his face. It smelled like rubber and farts.

"Whatever, Hugs," Brynn crossed her legs and closed her eyes. "We gonna meditate or what?"

"Positive language, Brynn." Huggy Bear turned and patted Dixie's knee. "And our new friend said that he would prefer not—"

"Meditation is good!" Dixie said, and folded his legs into the lotus position. He closed his eyes and smiled. Who knew therapy was such a great place to meet chicks?

The meditation wasn't so bad as Dixie expected. There was calm music, a soft place to sit, candles, and incense. He made a mental note to bring along some warm milk and a blanket for his next therapy session.

"Hey," a soft, sweet voice whispered into Dixie's ear. "Wake up!"

He opened his eyes. Brynn sat in front of him. Flashes of golden wheat shone out from the roots of her tangled, ink black hair. So, if this goth thing didn't work out, she could always grow out her hair and model for Swiss Miss hot chocolate. It was always good to have a back-up plan.

"Why are you here?" she asked.

Of course, that would also require some wardrobe modifications.

"I think we're supposed to be meditating."

Not an unpleasant prospect. Dixie imagined that she'd look quite fetching in some lederhosen and pigtails.

"Don't be an idiot."

"Yeah, but . . ." Dixie looked around Brynn's face to Huggy Bear's beanbag. His eyes were closed and his head tilted back. "It's just that . . ."

"You aren't worried about him, are you?"

Dixie shrugged. He'd never had to explain why he obeyed an authority figure before. It was just something he did.

"He's sleeping, dude," Brynn said.

"No, that's meditation," Dixie said. "He's just really good at it."

Brynn swiveled around to face Huggy Bear. "Hey, fruity!"

Huggy Bear didn't move. He was asleep. So, that's the secret to inner peace. No wonder the siesta-taking countries of the world were so mellow. Except Colombia, but Dixie was fairly certain that that was more the cocaine trade than anything else.

Brynn scooted forward onto Dixie's beanbag. "What are you here for?"

Dixie scooted back. "Uhh . . . possession of a controlled substance and assaulting a school employee."

"That was you?"

Dixie would have appreciated a little less surprise in her voice, but at least he got her attention, and that was the first step in any successful relationship.

"Yeah."

"So what was it, then?"

"Meth." At least he hoped it was—the headline would look much better that way.

"You do meth?"

"Something like that."

Brynn cocked an eyebrow and stared at Dixie. "You know that's a drug, right?"

"Oh, yeah," Dixie said and nodded. "I'm a junkie. Big time."

"Okay." Brynn smiled and then turned back toward her beanbag.

"Wait."

In hindsight, Dixie supposed that he should have stayed quiet. After all, he'd gone through the entirety of their conversation without suffering any major body malfunctions (pretty girls gave him nosebleeds), and he'd already used up all his good conversational material.

She turned back. "What?"

Dixie motioned toward the vending machine outside of the weight lifting trailer. "Do you wanna go halvesies on a pack of Rollos or something?"

He wasn't sure if that would exactly qualify as a date, but it was the most romance he could muster with the wrinkled dollar bill in his pocket.

Brynn lifted the corner of her mouth into a smile. "Freaking weird, dude."

"So, is that a no?" Dixie asked. "I'm pretty sure they have trail mix."

Brynn shook her head. "We should meditate."

"Okay," Dixie said and closed his eyes. It wasn't quite what he had been hoping for, but at least she hadn't called him a "homo" or kicked him in the shin.

"Welcome to therapy." Brynn's lips grazed across Dixie's ear on the last syllable, and then she shot up another stale breeze as she sat down in her beanbag.

"Whoa," Dixie whispered. He was fairly confident he had just gotten to first base. Maybe. He had never really been all that clear on the specifics. But sexual milestone or no, he couldn't let this take focus from his investigation. The hearing was only six days away, and there wouldn't be too many chances for romance if he got sent away to VisionQuest.

Dixie settled into his beanbag and reclined against the padded cover of the bench press. It was time to focus. He was starting his surveillance on the football team at the rally in a few hours, and he needed to prepare himself with a little relaxation and inward reflection. Hopefully with enough of both he could talk down his boner before the hour was up and Parksie returned to escort him back to the office. He was just starting out in his friendship with the man and didn't want to give him the wrong impression.

Chapter 11

Tuesday, 8:23 p.m.

"It's a tremendous honor to be the mistress of ceremonies for this year's night rally."

"Uh-huh." Dixie furrowed his brow into "interested journalist" mode and held his tape recorder under Julie's mouth. In addition to being the current record holder for the dead lift at Stilton High and the bane of his older brother's existence, Julie was also the mistress of ceremonies for the night rally, an honor usually reserved for girls who wanted another picture in the yearbook but weren't quite pretty enough to be nominated for homecoming queen.

This year was no exception.

He looked past the ridge of trapezius muscle jutting out of Julie's short, tight black dress (though Dixie assumed the designer's only intended adjective was "black") to the action on the field.

A varsity cheerleader buried her face in a kiddy pool full of Jell-O on the fifty-yard line, retrieved an apple with her teeth, then passed the fruit into the starting quarterback's mouth. Dixie assumed they were dating. It didn't seem like two people would do something like that unless there was some kind of substantial commitment in place, at least not in the middle of a football field with a few thousand people cheering in the stands.

The cheerleader dunked her face in the pool again and bit into another apple. The angle of her bend and the length of her legs caused her skirt to rise just enough for a clear view of her thong.

Dixie took a moment to admire the craftsmanship of the fine folks at Victoria's Secret and finally understood the allure of school spirit.

He tore his eyes from the thin, wonderful lace and looked across the field to the loose herd of football players milling around next to the goalpost. For a bunch of chemically altered psychopaths, they sure were a dull bunch to spy on. So far the only illegal activity that Dixie had observed was cheerleader molestation, but that was normal enough and didn't help his investigation into the meth cartel.

"I think it's really important for a person to give back to their school, and I love to perform. . . . I did ballet when I was a kid."

"Uh-huh." Dixie nodded at Julie and squished around the plastic grass and rubber turf to get a better angle on the jocks. The football field was made of a new high-tech material called Motion Turf, the same stuff that NFL teams put down in their stadiums and costs more by the square foot than weapons-grade plutonium. The whole thing seemed a bit extravagant to Dixie, but at least the plastic grass didn't stain his sneakers during PE. That seemed about worth the five-hundred-thousand-dollar investment. Textbooks and computers were overrated, anyway.

He looked past the football team to the floating embers and long shadows cast from the bonfire onto the softball field. The bonfire had been an unofficial staple of the night rally since the early 1940s, and though the school board was technically opposed to the rampant sexual harassment and underage drinking that were inevitable whenever teenagers were introduced to an open flame, it was difficult to completely eliminate something with that much history behind it. Especially when several hundred inebriated jocks wanted to burn stuff and fondle boobies. It was a compromise, really.

Dixie heard a string of steady thumps and a low rumble behind him. The football team was on the move. He turned to watch as the players marched in single file toward the bonfire, pounding out the cadence of their steps on the shoulder pads of the man in front with a surprisingly adept sense of rhythm. Dixie supposed that made sense; most of the jazz greats were junkies, too.

"Are you staring at my tits?"

Uh-oh.

It was at this moment Dixie realized that the football players shared an unfortunate sight line with Julie's cleavage. Though to be fair, so did almost everything else in the stadium.

"Uhh . . . I think I have enough for my article." Dixie lowered his recorder and shuffled back.

Julie looked Dixie up and down and sneered. "You're a pervert. Just like your brother."

"Sorry?" Dixie dropped his eyes and jogged to the safety of the track. It wasn't standard journalistic practice to run away from an interview subject, but Julie looked like she was about to maul him.

Dixie watched the football team disappear into the smoke and shadows next to the bonfire and followed in their wake. He was entering wild, dangerous territory, but like Nichols said, "a good investigative reporter follows his story no matter where it leads."

Besides, if Dixie heard "My Humps" one more time, he was going to have an aneurysm.

It wasn't quite so bad at the bonfire as Dixie anticipated. There was no body paint, ritual dancing, or animal sacrifice, but at least the Natural Ice consumption and miniskirts were at their expected levels. That was a comfort.

"Show us your tits! Show us your tits!"

Dixie looked over to the noise: a ring of silverbacks at the outskirts of the fire chanted at something in their center.

He walked to the circle. That could be Funt in there, and though it seemed a little homoerotic and strange to Dixie for them to get so frothed up over breasts of the male persuasion, he had to investigate every possible lead.

"Show us your tits!" Dixie joined in, and nosed his way into the center of the crowd. Nobody noticed. They were all too focused on the tits, and though he still didn't understand why they wanted Funt to take off his shirt, there was a certain charm to the group mentality.

Come on, Funt! Let's see those titties!

It wasn't Funt. Dixie was sure that he would have been much more disappointed if he weren't nipple level with the girl as she lifted up her blouse. He was fairly certain they had geometry together, but it was difficult to be sure with the inadequate lighting and bare breasts inches from his face.

Dixie looked at the outskirts of the circle and saw Brynn lift a wad of crumpled bills from the letterman jacket of one of the steak heads. She moved with surprising grace and stealth for a person wearing Doc Martens. She pocketed the cash and stepped back into the shadows before her target noticed the theft. Of course, with the distraction of the naked girl, she could have used the subtlety of a fungo bat to his knee and still achieved the same result, but impressive moxy, regardless.

"One, two, three . . . heave!"

Dixie backed out of the circle and turned to see a fireman's brigade of drunk jocks pass down a leather recliner and huck it onto the peak of the bonfire. Black smoke floated up from the leather and filled the air. It was probably some kind of hazard, but that didn't really matter. Even if the teachers and police officers standing by on the football field wanted to regain control, it was going to take a whole lot of manpower and tear gas, and if *Lord of the Flies* had taught the world anything, it was best to give the younger ones a wide berth after prolonged exposure to campfire.

"Any progress with the sodomy?"

Dixie smiled. He never thought he would be so happy to hear those words.

He turned around: Funt and the albino walked past the circle of "titty" chanters and around to the outskirts of the bonfire.

"What'd I tell you about that?" Funt asked.

Dixie stepped into the shadows and followed behind. He was glad to see that Funt and the albino had settled their differences; they'd need all the allies they could get once he sent them off to juvie.

"You did, didn't you?"

Funt and the albino stopped in front of a large tunnel covered in plastic tarp at the border between the bonfire and end zone. The line of jocks from the football field marched inside, and a fog machine pumped in smoke through a hose connected to the top.

Evidently the rally committee was planning to fill the tunnel with football players and then have them burst out through a cloud of smoke onto the field during the school fight song. That was always a crowd favorite. Nothing entertained a large group of morons quite like sweaty jocks, loud music, and a fog machine. Dixie understood that professional wrestling operated on a similar formula.

"Shut up." Funt walked to the tunnel entrance and started an elaborate hand-slap-fist-bump combo with the albino.

"Look, I'm not judging, here," the albino said. "That's God's responsibility."

"It's not a sin."

The hand slap continued. They were doing something with the tips of their fingers. Creepy.

"You should really take a break from all that sexual deviancy and read a few verses," the albino said. "It might help you with your confusion."

Wait a minute, that wasn't just any handshake—

"Fuck off," Funt said, and walked into the tunnel.

—That was a drug hand off.

"I'll miss you, honey." and the albino disappeared into the shadows.

Dixie stared at the tunnel. He didn't want to follow Funt inside. Going into a dark, enclosed space with a bunch of strung-out he-beasts went against every instinct. But like Rick said (and usually about Funt's mom), "It all looks the same in the dark," and that tunnel was just the cover Dixie needed to get close to his target.

He shot back a spray from his inhaler, then ran along the shadows to the side of the tunnel. He lifted up the anchoring spike, rolled under into the musty darkness, and pushed up to his feet before any large mammal stepped on his head.

"Go Wildcats!" Dixie crashed against the bodies to get further into the tunnel. "Go Wildcats!" And crashed again.

The bodies had a whole lot more give than Dixie expected from people who spent the majority of their waking hours injecting stimulants and lifting weights. They probably just gossiped and braided each other's hair, Dixie thought. You couldn't get three guys in the same room without it turning into a slumber party.

Dixie's fingers sunk into something particularly spongy, and he stopped. "Funt?"

"What?" the sponge asked.

"Are you Funt?"

"Nah, Brett." The sponge exhaled and popped out Dixie's fingers. "Who're you?"

"Javier." That was the team kicker, and the closest match to Dixie's body type and voice timbre from the available selection on the team.

"Oh," the sponge said. "Whassup?"

"Hey." The sponge wasn't Dixie's planned target, but he supposed that one meth addict worked just as well as any other. "I need some more of the stuff."

"What?"

"The stuff." Dixie nudged his elbow against the under cup of the sponge's left tit. "You know, the stuff stuff."

"What are you talking about, Javier?"

So, the sponge was playing dumb was he? Dixie was ready for that, too.

"I wanna bump the white pony."

"What?" the sponge asked. "What the hell does that mean?"

"I think he's trying to seduce you" a voice next to the sponge said.

"Dude, quit trying to seduce me!"

Dixie felt a hard push on his shoulder and fell back into a body behind him.

"Watch it!" the body said. Dixie stopped—there was something familiar about that voice.

"Rick?"

"Yeah."

Dixie kicked at the voice's projected crotch and connected with something solid. Maybe a shin. Maybe even Rick's.

"What the hell, Javier?"

The kick wasn't the right move journalistically. He still hadn't found out anything useful about the team's supplier, or scored another sample of the meth, but such a prime opportunity for sneak attack didn't come around too often, and Dixie wanted to take full advantage.

"Come here, you asshole!"

The key for next time was to think through a better exit strategy before kicking—the tunnel didn't leave much in the way of maneuverability.

Something pushed against Dixie's face and forced him to the ground.

And that was a bad place to be just then.

The school's fight song played, plastic ripped, the crowd screamed, feet stomped toward the brightness on the field, and down, and on, and . . .

There was pain and light and noise.

Then there was just pain.

And then there was none.

Chapter 12

Tuesday, 11:17 p.m.

"Mr. Nguyen?"

Dixie blinked into consciousness. The ceiling was white, his mouth was dry, and his neurons were playing tug-of-war with his optic nerves.

"Mr. Nguyen?"

He wasn't sure where he was or how he'd gotten there, but the sleeping surface was considerably more comfortable than the army cot at the school.

Dixie looked around to get a bearing on his location: blue paper pajamas, protective roll bars on the side of the bed, an odor like somebody took a dump in a can of bleach. . . . This was a hospital.

"Wake up, Mr. Nguyen."

Dixie felt a nudge on his shoulder and turned to the voice. A tall doctor with leathery skin and a ponytail stared back.

"How are you feeling, Mr. Nguyen?"

"Uhh . . . not so wonderful."

"Great. Follow with your eyes, please." The doctor leaned over the bed and moved his index finger back and forth in front of Dixie's face. "Good."

"Good what?"

The doctor walked to the foot of Dixie's bed and made a few notations on the chart. "There doesn't appear to be any lasting neurological damage."

"Neurological damage from what?"

"Apparently a football player stepped on your head."

"Oh." So, that wasn't just a bad dream.

"You suffered a mild concussion," the doctor continued. "Just don't sleep anymore for the next twelve hours, and you should be fine."

"Are you sure?" Dixie asked. "It's a school night."

The doctor stared down the ridge of his nose at Dixie. "Don't sleep for the next twelve hours, or you might fall into a coma and die."

"Check." That seemed like a solid enough reason to Dixie and nothing that a second cup of morning Ovaltine couldn't fix.

"Your family's waiting in the lobby, so go ahead and get dressed." The doctor walked to the door and stopped. "I'm sure your roommate won't mind."

"What?" Dixie asked. He looked through the open furl of curtain to his side. "Oh, sweet Jesus!"

His roommate was Dale.

The security guard didn't appear conscious and was weighted down with too much plaster and too many wires to pose much of an immediate threat, but Dixie still twisted his strong hand into a claw of death.

"Yeah . . ." The doctor paused at the doorway. "Poor guy. Some kid got hopped up on crank and mugged him."

"Shame." Dixie gulped and edged back across the mattress. "So, uhh . . . would you classify him as much of a threat at the moment?"

"What?"

"You know, vendettas . . . retaliatory strikes, anything like that?"

"No. He's knocked out on morphine and has a broken hip." The doctor stepped back into the room. "Are you sure you're feeling okay?"

"Yeah, it's just . . . drugs destroy lives and all that." Dixie leaned back and relaxed his claw of death. "Poor old guy."

"Right." The doctor stared at Dixie for a moment and then turned back into the hallway.

Dixie pushed himself up off the mattress, ignored the updraft along his southern equator, and grabbed the Jell-O cup off the tray of food by his bed.

"I'm sorry." Dixie stepped forward and set the cup on Dale's side table. He wasn't sure if Dale liked Jell-O, but it was the best he could manage at the moment.

He turned back to the closet at the back of the room and found his clothes on the hangers inside. Muddy cleat prints ran up the center of his jeans and shirt. Dixie sighed—Mrs. Presto would not be pleased come laundry day.

Dixie changed, checked his nostrils in the closet's mirror,

and noticed a familiar blue glint in the open crack of Dale's closet.

He swung open the closet door: Dale's crumpled denim shirt hung on a plastic hanger inside. Dixie grabbed the hanger and held the fabric up to the fluorescent light. A small prick of white shone through a puncture in the collar.

Bingo. That's where Dale got stabbed with the syringe, and unless they'd washed this at the hospital (from the smell of things, unlikely) there would still be traces of meth in the fabric. He just needed to figure out how to test the fabric for narcotics, and he could finally prove *what* the football players were taking.

He pulled the shirt off the hanger and smiled; this was a good time to live with a policeman. The sergeant parked his police cruiser in the family garage and kept a narcotic detection kit in the trunk. Well, at least that's what the police did on reality television, and Dixie didn't expect his father to be an exception. Judging by their facial hair and fondness for softball, the profession didn't seem to attract a lot of independent thinkers.

Dixie looked behind the open door to the empty corridor and stuffed the shirt down his pants. Dale wouldn't be needing this for a while, and besides, after all that he'd put the man through, the least Dixie could do was to get this dry-cleaned.

Chapter 13

Wednesday, 11:18 a.m.

The tardy bell rang, and Dixie shuffled to the back of the chemistry lab to claim his stool next to the eyewash station. He wasn't supposed to be there—banishment from class was the entire point of being suspended—and on any other day, Dixie would have welcomed the excuse to skip chemistry.

Today was different. Today, he was carrying a police-issued narcotics detection kit in his backpack and had an XL-denim meth sample to test.

Dixie set his backpack on the lab table and settled back in his chair. Sneaking into the classroom had been surprisingly easy (the system just wasn't designed to curb that particular flow of traffic), and unless his teacher, Mr. Stone, dropped his fantasy fiction book to inspect the ranks for intruders, he was safe.

It was almost too easy.

He would have preferred somewhere a bit more private to conduct the experiment, but there were only traces of meth in the fabric, and he needed the full use of the lab's facilities to observe the chemical reaction of the narcotic detection kit.

Dixie pulled the "community" microscope across the table and set it in front of his station. Unfortunately, that was the technological limit of the facilities. He imagined it was difficult to find much wiggle room for scientific equipment in the school budget when the new football field cost more than the GDP of Paraguay.

He heard low mutterings to his left and turned to the noise. His lab partner rustled a mini-doughnut out of its packaging and dangled it over the open flame of a Bunsen burner. It seemed like a waste of a perfectly good mini-doughnut to Dixie, but he supposed it was all for the best; Tubby didn't need the extra calories.

Tubby wasn't his real name. Well, at least Dixie assumed it wasn't; they still hadn't been formally introduced. That was okay, though; their three-month partnership as "lab buddies" worked just fine the way it was: Dixie did all the work, and Tubby mumbled to himself and burned stuff.

Mr. Stone swiveled around on his chair, wrote READ CH. 14 on the blackboard in broad strokes of chalk, and the class then took their cue to fall asleep or play Tetris on their cell phones. Dixie appreciated the silence. Today he was isolating trace narcotic elements from a heterogeneous compound, and the experiment required his full and undivided attention.

Isolating trace narcotic elements from a heterogeneous compound . . . that had a nice ring to it, and Dixie made a note of it in his binder. The science fair was just around the corner, and he didn't want to disappoint on his follow-up to last year's blue ribbon effort. Of course, when ninety percent of competing entries were baking-soda volcanoes, it tended to devalue the prestige of the award, but Dixie supposed it all looked the same on a college application.

He checked over both shoulders to make sure that no one was watching, then reached into his backpack for Dale's shirt and the small, plastic bottle of NARCOTIC DETECTION ACTIVATOR. At least that's what was written on the box he stole from the sergeant's police cruiser last night.

Dixie twisted the cap off the bottle and measured out a few ounces of the clear liquid into the attached dropper. It was the first time that he had ever stolen anything in his life. Dixie assumed that he might have felt a bit more guilty if the crime hadn't been so easy:

11:10 a.m.–12:47 a.m.: Get back from hospital. Wait for family to go to sleep (with an assist from Folgers instant coffee and the fine late-night programming on Animal Planet).

12:47 a.m.–12:49 a.m.: Walk to kitchen. Lift the sergeant's keys.

12:49 a.m.–12:58 a.m.: Walk to garage. Cycle through trunk of police cruiser. Steal narcotic detection kit.

Dixie laid the collar across the microscope's viewing tray and positioned the dropper over the puncture wound in the collar. According to the instructions on the side of the bottle, "after two minutes, the liquid will turn red in the presence of a narcotic."

He basted the liquid onto the puncture in the collar and cranked down on the magnification wheel until the denim came into focus.

He set his watch, stuck his eye into the nozzle of the microscope, and waited for the liquid to work its magic.

Thirty seconds: no change in fabric.

Sixty seconds: no change in fabric. Slight odor of smoke.

Ninety seconds: no change in fabric. Strong smell of smoke.

"Oh no!"

Ninety-three seconds: no change in fabric. Strong smell of smoke. Fire alarm goes off.

Dixie twisted his eyeball loose from the lens and looked up: the sleeves of Dale's shirt were draped over Tubby's Bunsen burner. Yellow licks of flame danced up the collar, and a trickle of black smoke swirled up toward the ceiling.

Tubby jumped off his stool and pointed at the fire. "Holy crap!"

This was bad.

Dixie stared at the small puffs of smoke rising from the shirt, and a series of plans flashed through his mind:

1. Wait for fire to burn out. Apologize. Hope for the best.

2. Grab scissors from supply drawer. Take Tubby as a hostage. Demand helicopter from police.

3. Run.

He stared across the lane of desks to the open door on the other side of the room. It was probably best to go with option three; he found that the simplest solution usually worked best in these kinds of situations.

So, while the rest of the class cheered the licks of yellow flame spreading across the denim, and Mr. Stone struggled to dislodge the fire extinguisher from the wall mount, Dixie swept the remains of the narcotic detection kit into his backpack and bolted out of the room.

He hated to leave the evidentiary base of his investigation smoldering on the table, but that fire was the perfect diversion to cover his escape, and besides, he had watched enough *CSI* to realize that forensic evidence usually didn't do so well when exposed to an open flame.

Dixie sprinted around the edge of the chemistry building and ducked through the underbrush into the woods that infested the back property of the campus. He tried to avoid the place as much as possible. Not only were there the standard tick/mountain lion/backpacking hippie concerns, but this was also the established territory for the freaky goth kids at Stilton High and the preferred location for the smoking, sexual deviancy, and mascara application that took up most of their day.

But there were a few things that made Dixie ignore this usual safeguard—

He vaulted over a low bush, veered around a tangle of used condoms, and pushed farther into the tree cover.

—And fleeing from a crime scene was one of them.

Dixie's sneaker stubbed into an exposed tree root, and he skidded across the damp leaves and cigarette butts into a small clearing. This seemed like just as good a place as any to take a break.

He rolled onto his back and whispered a string of hot

profanity into his chest. He would have preferred to shout the curse words and maybe even punch a tree stump for good measure, but he didn't want to chance an asthma attack, and the broken knuckles wouldn't make him feel that much better, anyway.

He had just lost the story. There was no more meth sample. There was nothing to connect the football team to the drugs. There was no way to prove his innocence at the hearing on Monday.

He had nothing.

He was going to VisionQuest.

He was screwed.

Dixie grabbed an empty bottle of wine cooler off the ground and hucked it at the nearest tree—he was running out of creative variations on the F word, and it just felt appropriate for the moment. The bottle hit the tree with a light thunk and bounced back into the tall grass.

Dixie sighed. He'd been hoping for something a bit more cathartic. Perhaps he'd needed a running start.

"Hey."

Dixie yipped and turned to the voice: Brynn leaned against a tree on the outskirts of the clearing, smoking a cigarette.

"Uhh . . . hi." Dixie coughed to cover the high-pitched noise he had just squealed.

Brynn flicked the stub of her cigarette into the damp leaves. "You throw like a chick."

Dixie nodded; Tee Ball had been an especially difficult few months. "I kinda need some alone time."

Before this moment, Dixie had never imagined that he would have willingly passed on the chance to spend time with a girl, and especially one that was so pretty, and easy to talk to and just mentally damaged enough that he might even have an outside chance at romance. But this had been a particularly emotional afternoon, and though Dixie didn't have much experience with girls, he was fairly certain that curling into a ball and weeping wasn't the best way to start the seduction process.

Brynn walked over and stood next to Dixie. "Rough day, huh?"

"Something like that." Dixie readjusted his glasses. "I'm emotionally complicated."

That might have been a bit of a stretch, but Dixie understood that women found that alluring in a man, and it was a whole lot easier than developing stomach muscles or buying a truck.

"Really?" Brynn stifled a chuckle and nodded her head. "So, is there anything I can do to help?"

"No, probably not," Dixie said. "Not unless you know where I can score some more meth or catch a fast train to Venezuela."

"What?"

"Venezuela?" Dixie pushed up to his feet and knocked the loose dirt off his pants. "It's a country in South America . . . loose extradition laws. Forget it."

"I know where Venezuela is, asshole," Brynn said, and flipped her bangs out of her eyes. "So, you want some meth, huh?"

Dixie looked down at his shoes. "Yeah . . . I love that meth."

"My boyfriend's a bartender up at the Old Dog House. He sells crank, if you need any." She looked up at Dixie and smiled. "You know, since you're such a junkie and all."

"Uhh . . . great." Dixie felt a cold lump drop in his stomach. So, she had a boyfriend, did she? That was disappointing. But if he wanted to land a high quality girl like Brynn, he supposed that some competition was inevitable. Some old, scary, drug dealing competition.

"Hey, would you mind not telling Huggy Bear about this?" Brynn pulled another cigarette out of her leather jacket and flicked open the flame on her lighter. "He's kinda sensitive about the whole enabling thing."

"You got it." Dixie leaned his arm against a moss-covered tree trunk and hoped that the appearance of nonchalance was worth chancing the allergic reaction. "So, uhh . . . you come here often?"

Sure, she was technically "spoken for" or whatever, but Dixie didn't see the harm in laying down a little groundwork. He doubted that meth-dealing statutory rapists really made for the best long-term boyfriend material.

"Real smooth, jackass." Brynn stepped out of the clearing, but turned back before she left. The corner of her mouth lifted into a smirk. "Just try not to overdose before therapy tomorrow, okay? I like the company."

Dixie nodded and gave her a thumbs-up. "I'll just take enough to stay normal."

"Freaking weird, dude." Brynn spiked the cigarette

between her lips and pushed through a manzanita thicket onto the faint dirt trail that led back to the school.

Dixie watched her disappear into the shadows and smiled. Maybe things weren't quite so bad, after all. The hearing was less than a week away, and he had just burned his only evidence, but that was okay. He had an even better lead now: Brynn's boyfriend, aka the statutory rapist, aka the bartender at the Old Dog House, aka the leading candidate for the meth kingpin of Stilton County.

Plus, somewhere between the insults and the cigarettes, he was certain Brynn had been flirting with him. Yep, there was a whole lot of good that had just happened in the last few minutes.

Dixie lowered himself down onto a relatively dry spot under a tree and snuggled his face against the soft pouch of his backpack. So, all that left was figuring out how to sneak out of his house, travel across the county, and go undercover as a meth addict in the most dangerous bar in Northern California, and his investigation would be right back on track. This was a whole lot easier when he was just pouring chemicals on some denim.

He brushed a wet leaf off his cheek, set his digital watch for a fifteen-minute power nap, and closed his eyes. He didn't expect to get much sleep tonight and like Nichols said, "There's no force more powerful than a fully rested journalist."

Chapter 14

Wednesday, 10:38 p.m.

Dixie pressed his ear against his bedroom wall and waited for the sounds of seagulls and humpback whales to vibrate through the thin plaster from his parents' bedroom.

He counted down sixty seconds on his watch and stepped back from the wall. The sergeant was supervising the graveyard shift, Brandon was out gluing sparkles, or some such idiocy for the homecoming float, and Mrs. Presto would remain under the spell of her soothing ocean sounds CD and two glasses of Chablis until her 7:30 a.m. water aerobics class.

Dixie opened his notebook to the night's planning sheet and crossed a line through Phase One: wait for Mom to fall asleep.

Now, onto Phase Two: final disguise inspection.

Dixie looked in his closet mirror and checked to make sure that his outfit properly conveyed "alcoholic lumberjack." It wasn't the most professional disguise, but it was the best he could manage from a box of old Halloween costumes in the back of his closet. Hopefully the mass intoxication and indirect lighting at the bar would smooth out the rest of the rough edges. There were several elements to the ensemble:

1. Fake beard. Halloween 1999, Hobo. The nylon strands irritated his skin, and didn't allow for much ventilation, but he needed something to distract from his boyish good looks.

2. Earring. Halloween 2003, Gentleman Pirate. Or, in the words of his father, a "Homosexual."

3. Trucker hat. Spring 2004. Well, that wasn't part of a costume so much as an unsuccessful attempt to latch on to the Von Dutch fashion craze. Adolescence is a confusing time.

4. X-small plaid shirt. Summer 1997, Camping trip. It was a bit tight around the chest by now, and didn't quite stretch down to cover all of his torso, but it was the most rugged piece of clothing in his wardrobe.

Dixie readjusted the fake beard's breathing aperture over his mouth, spit the loose fibers off his tongue, and crossed Phase Two off the sheet. He was ready.

He flicked off his light and tiptoed through the house to the garage. He moved the extra bags of kitty litter and toilet paper stacked in the corner to find the lynchpin of his operation:

Phase Three: steal Mom's bike.

Sure, it was a little rusty, and the pink-on-yellow color scheme didn't do much to accentuate his masculinity, but the bar was miles away, and this was the most reliable transportation available. Plus, the wire basket on front was sure to be handy for extra storage.

Speaking of extra storage.

He grabbed a box of Capri Suns off a wire shelf by the door and dumped them into the basket. He had a feeling those electrolytes would come in handy before the night was through.

Dixie wheeled the bike out the side door and, after several false starts and some light bruising on his left knee, wobbled down the street toward downtown. He still hadn't figured out how he was going to sneak into the Old Dog House and question the bartender, but there was still a long, uphill bike ride ahead, and he needed something to distract his mind from the inevitable chafing.

He turned down a grade, swerved around the loose pinecones on the asphalt, and half a mile later, skidded to a stop at the four-way intersection by the high school. A truck edged out from the opposite lane and stopped in the middle of the road.

Dixie stared into the intersection, and though it was difficult to distinguish much through the glare of headlights, there was something familiar about that truck. Of course, in a town where ninety percent of the population proudly owned and operated a late-model Ford, it was a common feeling.

But there was still something. . . .

The truck backed up a few feet and the passenger window rolled down in jerky, squeaky jumps. "Dixie?"

Dixie reached up to make sure that his disguise hadn't

blown off from the wind resistance. Nope, still there.

The interior lights of the truck flashed on: it was Brandon.

"What are you doing?" his brother asked.

Dixie pulled the visor of his cap down over his eyes. "Move along, mister."

"What are you wearing?" Brandon asked. "Jesus, Dixie, we talked about this."

"You were supposed to be working on the float," Dixie said, soft and low into his chest.

"We ran out of sparkles," Brandon said, and slapped down on the dashboard. "Now get in the goddamn truck!"

Dixie lowered his eyes and gripped the handlebars. He was caught. This was a delicate situation, and required an equal dose of finesse and sensitivity—

"Eat one!" Dixie angled his bike past the truck and threw his weight against the pedals.

—Or, failing that, the element of surprise and a fast bike.

"Dixie! Get back here! Godammit!"

Dixie swerved around a parked Volvo and turned down the road toward the high school. He couldn't keep up this pace for much longer, but he didn't need to outrun the truck, just get into the woods behind the school before he was forced off the road. The truck couldn't follow him up there, and as long as he kept heading straight and didn't impale himself on any manzanita, he was sure to pop out onto the main road, eventually.

The truck's horn blared and Brandon revved the engine. "Get off that goddamn bike or I'm gonna kick your ass!"

Dixie spotted a clear path into the wilderness, aimed his wheel toward the dirt embankment, and braced for the uphill climb to freedom.

Unfortunately, he forgot to account for the curb.

Dixie pretzeled the front wheel against the asphalt, flipped over the handlebars, and one-and-a-half rotations later, skidded to a halt against a tree stump.

This complicated the escape plan.

He took a moment to make sure nothing was broken or puncturing his lungs, then resumed his scramble up the embankment and into the woods on foot. Unfortunately, Dixie was only a few strides into the wilderness before he was hit with a painful realization: Brandon could leave the truck. Of course, it would have been nice if this painful realization hadn't coincided with the physical pain of his brother's tackle.

"I'm gonna kill you, Dixie!"

Dixie strained against the dirt to look up at his attacker. Brandon's face was red and clenched and his right fist was tucked in the firing chamber against his armpit.

"I know you're angry" Dixie said. "But if you punch me in the back of the head, you're gonna break your hand."

Dixie closed his eyes and braced for impact—but instead, he felt the pressure on his shoulders ease.

"What the hell is the matter with you?" Brandon asked.

"Nothing. I'm a drug addict, right?" Dixie squirmed against his brother's grip. "I'm gonna sell mom's bike for a bottle of glue. Now get off me!"

"Shut up." Brandon pushed Dixie's head against the

dirt. "Why are you out here? Are you in trouble?"

Dixie took a deep breath. He had hoped it wouldn't come to this. He had promised himself that he would never repeat what he saw in the coatroom at his Uncle Tommy's New Year's party while he was searching the house for an unoccupied toilet, but this was a desperate situation.

"If you don't get off me, I'm gonna tell Mom you made out with cousin Suzy."

Dixie felt the figure above him go tense and still for several seconds. He had long suspected there would be advantages to having a shy bladder and an inquisitive mind.

"What?"

"You heard me. I saw you two in Uncle Tommy's coatroom . . . shameful."

"She's a third cousin. . . . That's not even a blood relative."

"Whatever, sinner," Dixie said. "Now get off me or I'm gonna drop a Roosevelt dime on your ass."

Dixie wasn't sure what that meant exactly but had heard it in a movie once and hoped for a similar reaction.

He didn't get it.

"Fuck you!" Brandon lifted his fist up to his armpit and slammed it down against Dixie's skull.

The punch didn't hurt quite so much as Dixie had anticipated. Brandon had neither the clearance to get his hips into the attack nor the money to buy a class ring.

Dixie rubbed the back of his head and watched his brother stabilize his injured fist between his thighs and roll in the dirt. "I told you not to do that."

Brandon stopped rolling and stared at Dixie. "The next one's going to your nose."

"Fair enough." Dixie scooted back to a safe distance. "I should probably get going, anyway."

The color faded from Brandon's face, and he gulped back the lingering venom. "You're never gonna stop, are you?"

"What? You mean with the investigation?" Dixie shook his head. "No. No way, dude. I'm innocent."

Brandon stared at Dixie for a moment, then squeezed the bridge of his nose. "Okay."

"Okay, what?"

"I'll help you with whatever the hell it is you're trying to do. Just . . . you gotta promise to be careful, okay?"

Dixie hated to lie to his brother, especially now that he had extended such a sweet gesture, but "careful" just wasn't part of the job description.

"Very careful." Dixie smiled and reached out for a high five. "Glad to have you on the team."

"Sure." Brandon reluctantly completed the hand slap. "So, what now?"

Dixie stood up and brushed the dirt off the seat of his pants. "You're gonna drive me to the Old Dog House."

"The Old Dog House?" Brandon closed his eyes and resumed the death grip on his nasal cavity. "Look, if you want to get drunk, there're easier ways."

"It's for the investigation, silly." Dixie walked out of the clearing and clapped Brandon on the shoulder as he passed. "Hurry up. Last call's in two hours."

"You're crazy."

Dixie slid down the dirt embankment and power lifted his mom's bike into the back of the truck. Maybe Brandon was right. Maybe he was a little crazy, but he was crazy with a head full of dreams and a personal driver—

"Hurry up, Brandon!" Dixie reached the truck's open window and honked the horn. "Time's a-wasting."

—And if that was good enough for Mariah Carey, it was good enough for him.

Chapter 15

Wednesday, 11:24 p.m.

Fifteen minutes and one trip to the gas station for a restorative slushy later, the Presto family truck cruised past the Stilton city limits into Templeton, the home of the Old Dog House. At one time, the town had been the hub of lumber operations for the California foothills, but since the mill closed, Templeton had spiraled into depression and seediness.

Dixie avoided the place as much as possible. And beyond the annual trip to the Lumberjack Jubilee to watch any number of his relatives compete in the tug-of-war, he was successful. The Jubilee was always a disappointment: no cotton candy, the judges were too literal in their selection of the "lumberjack queen," and despite all the buildup for the tug-of-war, if Dixie wanted to be near a bunch of drunk people sweating on each other, he would have danced at his uncle's wedding.

As the truck rolled past the boarded up storefronts and

abandoned houses, Dixie stared down the main drag to the distant lights of the Old Dog House. No sign marked the establishment; it didn't need one. The assortment of rusted-out trucks angled next to the sidewalk was advertisement enough. Evidently alcohol and meth distribution was a recession-proof business.

Dixie pointed to a spot of darkness in the park across from the bar. "Go to the other side of the park."

Brandon didn't acknowledge the order but drove through the empty streets, angled the truck next to a picnic table, and killed the engine.

"Look, Dixie . . ." Brandon closed his eyes and took a deep breath. "I don't know why you're doing this, but it's stupid and dangerous, and don't do it, okay? I won't tell Mom and Dad about the other stuff."

Dixie checked his disguise in the rearview mirror and swiveled his cap into alignment. Brandon's offer was tempting, but he couldn't give up now. Not when he was so close to cracking this lead and proving his innocence.

"You got a magazine or something?" Dixie asked, and pushed open the door. "This might take a while."

Brandon slammed his head back into the cushioned neck support of his seat. "If you get hurt, I'm gonna kill you."

"Don't worry." Dixie stepped outside and pulled down the beard. "I have a plan."

That last part wasn't strictly true, but Dixie didn't want his brother to worry. He didn't have a plan—just a fake beard, a trucker's hat, and a whole lot of moxy. Hopefully, that would be enough.

Dixie walked through the park, tiptoed across the street, and took cover behind a trash can to monitor the security procedures at the bar's font door.

"What are you doing?"

Dixie tensed and turned toward the voice: a large man with ink black hair and a tan jacket stood next to the trash can. It was at this moment that Dixie reexamined his surroundings and decided that in future sneaking operations, it was probably best to avoid lingering under direct lighting.

"What's it look like?" Dixie said in the gruffest, most threatening voice he could muster. "I dropped my chaw."

"Sure thing, sport." The man chuckled and pushed into the bar. Slow country music and a dim red light leaked into the night air in the brief interval between open and closed door.

Dixie released his body's accumulated shivers and pulled himself to his feet. His disguise had just passed its first test. And though he would have preferred a bit more respect in the man's tone, just so long as it wasn't a kick to the nuts or a call to the police, he considered it well within the acceptable limits of success. He crossed the sidewalk and pushed open the bar door. Now came the difficult part.

Inside the bar it was dark and only slightly less depressing than a coal miner's wake, but thankfully the patrons were far too focused on staring through their drinks and contemplating suicide to pay much attention to the comings and goings at the front door.

Dixie scanned the room for the bartender. After several seconds of searching, he spotted a relatively vibrant specimen standing next to several shelves full of booze playing a late model Game Boy.

Dixie stepped closer. The bartender was tall and skinny with pockets of greasy hair sprouting around the perimeter of his lips that probably looked something like a mustache from the right distance.

He approached the bar, perched on an empty stool, and knocked on the counter. "Barkeep."

The bartender shifted his attention from the Game Boy to the unfamiliar voice. He stared at Dixie for a moment, then his frown twisted into a smirk. "Cute hat."

Dixie responded with a grunt. It wasn't quite proper manners, but "Why, thank you" and a curtsy didn't feel right, either.

"You want something?" the bartender asked.

"Whiskey."

The bartender tilted up the eastern ridge of his unibrow. "You sure?"

"Look, if I wanted to answer a bunch of stupid questions, I'd still be married to my first wife," Dixie said, though it was difficult for him to hear the words over the loop of *oh sweet merciful Buddha, please work* running through his head.

The bartender studied Dixie for a moment, chuckled, and then filled a shot glass from a black bottle on the shelf.

Dixie watched the bartender slide the glass across the counter. He smiled under the cover of his beard; this was going great! The bartender had already bought his disguise and accepted his presence. All that left was gaining his trust and pumping him for some information about the meth trade. At this rate he could still make it back home in time for Conan's monologue. Maybe this investigative reporter racket wasn't so difficult, after all.

"Something wrong?" the bartender asked.

"What?"

The bartender pointed to the shot glass. "Ain't you gonna drink it?"

Dixie stared at the oily brown liquid in his glass and felt a drop of cold sweat trail down his back. Perhaps he started that internal celebration a touch prematurely. "Sure."

He took a deep breath, offered a quick prayer to the gods of acid reflux, and splashed the whiskey through the beard's breathing hole.

"Blahh!" Dixie slammed the empty glass onto the counter and suppressed the regurgitation reflex. So, that's what whiskey tasted like. He didn't expect the bouquet to be quite so reminiscent of Tabasco and gasoline. Perhaps this was a bad vintage.

"What's the matter?" the bartender asked.

"Huh?" Dixie asked, and quickly realized that his face was situated unusually close to his right ear. "Uhh . . . muscle tic. I got bit by a rat in Vietnam."

At least that's how he'd heard the school's janitor explain away his shaky hands. Though after looking around the bar, Dixie now suspected the true origin of the janitor's malady was better explained by the fact that he was currently passed out in the pretzels three stools down.

"You were in Vietnam?"

"Yep," Dixie said. It was a nice change to tell the truth.

The bartender smirked and poured another shot of whiskey into Dixie's glass. "No vet pays for his booze here."

Dixie considered a polite refusal but decided against it. Passing on free alcohol would arouse too much suspicion in this crowd. "Thanks."

The bartender grabbed a thin plastic straw from behind the counter and dropped it into Dixie's glass. "This might help."

So, that's how the hairier specimens took their booze; Dixie didn't expect alcoholic lumberjacks to be so practical. "Obliged."

"To the war hero." The bartender filled a shot glass from another bottle under the counter, clinked it against Dixie's glass, and put it back in one smooth lift and gulp.

Dixie angled the straw into his mouth and sucked down the booze as fast as the thin plastic and the power of his lungs would allow—there was no way that it could taste worse than the first time.

It did.

He wiped the accumulated moisture off his beard and felt the whiskey's slow deterioration of his esophagus. The taste was still horrible enough, but at least the urge to vomit had somewhat dissipated. That was something like "better," right?

Dixie slammed his shot glass onto the table and hiccupped. Time to get to work. "So, you know where a fella can score some good horse 'round these parts—" Dixie started but quickly closed his mouth to cork off the mounting pressure bubbling up from his stomach. He supposed that the average customer would have gone ahead and belched, but he was pretty sure that a couple ounces of bile and recycled slushy would've stowed along for the ride.

The moment passed, and Dixie leaned in to resume his questioning.

"Like, I was saying, about the horse—" There was a series of splashes and clinks. Dixie looked down. His shot glass was full of whiskey again and flanked by two more of the same.

This was bad.

"Hold that thought, Rambo. There's someone here you've gotta meet." The bartender picked up a martini olive and threw it at the comatose janitor. "Hey, Barry! Wake up!"

So, his name was Barry; Dixie had always assumed he just went by Creepy Janitor.

Barry lifted his head from the table, a shard of pretzel stuck to his cheek. "What?"

The bartender slid the third shot glass down the bar. "On the house, buddy."

Barry picked up the glass and took a discriminating sniff. "I'm not drinking this crap."

"Show some gratitude." The bartender pointed at Dixie and winked. "It's for a fellow veteran."

Barry looked at Dixie, smiled, then slid off his stool. It was the first time that Dixie had ever seen the man express a positive emotion. Of course, if he spent eight hours a day wrist deep in Ty-D-Bowl and ketchup stains, Dixie wouldn't be much for grins and rainbows, either.

Dixie looked down at his shot glass, then back at the

janitor. This next bit was going to be awkward. It was best he didn't have all his wits about him, just then. He slammed down the whiskey and pushed the empty glass across the counter. "One more, here."

"Whoa, slow down there, buddy." The bartender tipped more whiskey into Dixie's glass. "There's still a bar full of guys that want to buy you a round."

Yippee.

"What company were you in?"

Dixie turned and found Barry standing a good eight inches inside his comfort bubble. On the good news side, the man smelled much fresher than Dixie expected from a drunkard custodian.

"To Jane Fonda, the whore!" Dixie lifted his glass to the janitor and threw it back in one gulp.

"Hoorah!" Barry lifted his shot glass toward his mouth but tipped the top third of his cargo onto Dixie's neck during transport. "Sorry . . . I was bit by a rat in Vietnam, you see." Barry dried his hand against the front of his shirt and belched stale Michelob into Dixie's face. "That's why my hands shake."

Dixie breathed the octane of Barry's words and nodded. Sure it is, buddy, sure it is.

"Funny you should say that." The bartender looked at Dixie and smiled. "It seems a rat bit our new friend here, too. Say, what is your name, friend?"

The repetition of "friend" made Dixie uncomfortable. No, actually it was the creepy janitor caressing his neck that made him uncomfortable. The "friend" thing was just disturbing.

"Dix—" Dixie froze before he blurted out the rest. It was probably best not to use his Christian name while on an undercover operation. "Uhh . . . Brick. Brick McGirt."

"Yeah, old Brick Dick here's got some rat problems, too." The bartender leaned close and winked. "Ain't that right, Dick?"

Dixie dropped his eyes from the bartender's penetrating gaze and muttered something along the lines of "yes" into his chest. He was beginning to suspect that this operation was taking a turn for the worse.

"Goddamn rats!" Barry shouted and sprayed into Dixie's ear. "So, where'd you do your hump, anyway?"

Dixie stared at the black bottle on the counter. He was starting to appreciate the nuances of sweet Kentucky mash.

He grabbed the bottle, but a stronger pair of hands pulled it back before he could siphon off any booze.

"Manners, Dick, manners," the bartender said, putting the bottle back onto the shelf. "We aren't in the jungle, anymore."

"I think this guy's beard's fake." Barry pulled on the synthetic hair and snapped the elastic support.

The beard fell off Dixie's face and settled onto the counter. His cover was compromised—but the free circulation of air against his face was a nice change.

The bartender picked the beard up and held it in front of Dixie's face. "You about finished?"

"I've got a medical condition," Dixie said.

"Look, it's been fun and all, but I'm done playing

around," the bartender said. "One more violation and I lose my license."

Barry leaned in close and sniffed Dixie's neck. "Hey, aren't you the kid who keeps losing his retainer?"

Dixie brushed Barry aside and turned to the bartender. His cover was blown, his subject was hostile, and the alcohol was sabotaging his higher reasoning functions. That just left him one chance to remedy this situation—

"Okay, you got me . . . I'm not really Brick McGirt." Dixie took off his hat and unclipped his earring. "I'm really a football player. I lost my weekly supply of the 'stuff' in my locker, and I don't want coach to get mad at me, so I figured I'd just go straight to the source and get some more . . . I've got five dollars."

—And if he was better at lying, or at least sober enough to maintain basic logic, it might have even worked.

The bartender picked up the glasses and dropped them into a sink behind the counter. "I have no idea what you're talking about."

"You know, the 'stuff.'" Dixie reached across the counter and nudged the bartender on the shoulder. "The stuff stuff."

The bartender smacked Dixie's hand off his shoulder, grabbed his shirt, and pulled him close. He was an Aqua Velva man.

"Are you freaking retarded, or are you just really trying to piss me off?"

"Uhh . . . neither?"

"Then explain to me what the hell you're talking about,

and if you say 'stuff' again, we're gonna have problems. You got that?"

Dixie nodded, or at least it was as close to a nod as he could manage with the pressure on his collar. "Sure."

"Good." The bartender released the fabric, and Dixie fell back onto the bar stool. "Now, what do you want?"

"One order of meth, please. Sir."

The bartender's face tightened with rage, and small red veins flared in his eyes.

"I don't sell that garbage, anymore." He reached into his shirt, and Dixie braced for a sharp object in his sternum to follow. Instead, the bartender fished out a small, wooden crucifix. "Not since I found the Lord."

Dixie stared at the cross for a moment and then winked; this was clearly some kind of insider code. "Okay, then . . . I'd like an extra large bag of communion wine."

"Don't mock the Lord, you little cock bag." The bartender dropped the crucifix back into his shirt. "I haven't touched crank in ten months. Go on somewhere else if you want that poison."

Dixie closed one eye, fixed his bullshit detector on the bartender, and sighed: he wasn't lying. The bartender wasn't the meth kingpin, just the worst Christian in the history of organized religion.

Well, this was depressing news. It was a good thing Dixie had found such a great new way of dealing with that. "Can I have some more whiskey, then?"

The bartender shook his head, reached behind the cash register, and dropped a large wrench onto the counter.

Dixie stared at the wrench and nodded. "Or, maybe I'll just be shuffling along."

He hopped off the stool and took a few steps toward the door, but his body felt an uncontrollable impulse to follow the tilt of the room toward the appetizing selection of potato salads on the buffet table in the center of the room.

Dixie raised his hands to protect his face from the serving forks, but a surer pair of hands grabbed him by the shoulders, steadied his equilibrium before disaster, and toted him fast and direct to the exit.

"Thanks for the help, but I got it from here. . . ." Dixie said over his shoulder but lost his train of thought somewhere between the toss at the door and his tumble across the sidewalk.

"And take your stupid freakin' carpet with you!"

Dixie looked up: the bartender threw his beard onto the sidewalk and then turned back to the open door.

"Wait!" Dixie yelled. His undercover assignment was ruined, but the night didn't have to be a total waste.

The bartender stopped. "What?"

"Just how serious are you and Brynn, anyway?"

The bartender stared down at Dixie and spit. "You tell that little slut to stop calling me . . . and if you ever come back here, I'm gonna make you eat that goddamn beard!"

"Does that mean she's single?" Dixie asked, but the bartender disappeared before he could answer.

The door swung closed, and Dixie rolled onto his back to watch the slow revolution of the neon beer advertisement in the bar's window. He hadn't found the meth kingpin, or anything else useful for his investigation, but at least it sounded like Brynn and the bartender were going through a rough patch. That's good—Dixie was in perfect position for her emotional rebound.

A flood of light crawled over the sidewalk. An engine shuddered and a car door slammed.

"Oh crap! Oh crap! Oh crap!"

Dixie rolled over and looked toward the noise.

"Dixie!" His brother jumped out of the truck. "Are you okay?"

"Yeah, I'm great." Dixie tilted his face away from the glare of the headlights and smiled. "There were a few snags with the undercover work. Hey, have you ever tried whiskey? It's fantastic!"

"Huh?" Brandon sniffed the exhaust from Dixie's mouth. "Are you drunk?"

"Probably . . . Hey, so it turns out Brynn's single. Isn't that awesome? Wait, did I ever tell you about Brynn? Excuse me . . ."

Dixie's stomach erupted, releasing the excess whiskey, stomach juice, and cherry Slurpee.

"Come on!"

Unfortunately, Dixie failed to notice that Brandon's sneakers were in the epicenter of the spray zone.

"Oh . . . sorry, dude." Dixie reached over to clean the chunks off Brandon's sneakers, but then the edges of his world turned a little gray, a little black, and it suddenly seemed like a much more pressing concern to take a nap.

* * *

Dixie opened his eyes and stared down at a sizable mound of vomit and black pavement. Somewhere, something metal pounded against something slightly less metal and just slightly off rhythm with the throbs of lava behind his eyeballs. Dixie assumed that had something to do with all the whiskey. Also the nausea.

Speaking of nausea . . .

Well, at least that explained the puddle of vomit.

Dixie twisted around and examined his surroundings. He was in the sergeant's truck, positioned lengthwise across the front bench with his head sticking out the passenger's door. It was a clever arrangement: he was safe from asphyxiating on his own vomit, and the truck's interior was safe from any unsightly stains.

He grabbed the steering wheel and pulled himself up to a sitting position. The exact details of the last few hours were still a bit hazy (something about a fake beard and bicycles, and there was definitely a liberal amount of whiskey in there), but he was fairly certain that his brother had orchestrated this last bit. Also, Brandon was probably the reason that Dixie wasn't currently shivering to death in some dark corner of Templeton.

Dixie wiped his mouth off against his shirt and made a mental note to give his brother a thank-you Otter Pop just as soon as his investigation was finished. He had certainly earned it.

He scooted out of the driver's door and examined the large, empty expanse of asphalt and perpendicular lines. He was in a parking lot, either the high school or Wal-Mart. Dixie hoped it was the high school. He was in no condition to deal with "Everyday Low Prices" at the moment.

Dixie followed the noise across the parking lot and into the open door of the school bus maintenance garage. Brandon stood on top of the senior class float, nailing green and yellow streamers to the back wall. He was sweaty, pale, and covered in green paint. It wasn't a good look for him.

He turned and looked down at Dixie. "Feeling better?"

"A little," Dixie said, if having puked out everything not stapled to his skeleton could be considered better.

"Good." Brandon bent over and grabbed another nail from a pile on the floor. "I called Mom. . . . she thinks you've been helping me on the float. I'll take you back home in a bit."

Dixie nodded. "Thanks."

Brandon stuck a nail through a strand of yellow streamer. "It's cool."

Dixie stared at the red lines and flecks of paint below his brother's eyes. He really was a nice guy. All Brandon did tonight was help, and what did Dixie do in return? Well, he was pretty sure that he had puked on Brandon's shoes at some point, and that alone was dicked enough to feel bad for the guy.

"So, you need some help?" Dixie asked.

Brandon wiped a stream of sweat off his forehead with the back of his hand. "You promise not to puke on anything?"

"I'll do my best."

"Grab a hammer, then."

Dixie smiled, stepped up onto the ladder, and stopped. He had almost forgotten the most important part.

"You got any aspirin?"

Chapter 16

Thursday, 2:10 p.m.

"Go in peace, young friend."

Dixie nodded at Huggy Bear and stumbled down the ramp of the weight lifting trailer into the wind chill and bright sunshine outside. He never thought such a thing was possible, but he had actually enjoyed his therapy session. Well, at least the twenty minutes he got to nap during meditation. The "feelings" and "affirmation" talk was just as horrifying as usual, but Dixie was willing to endure just about anything for some quiet time on the beanbag.

It had been a difficult morning.

The float construction hadn't finished until 7:48 a.m., which left just enough time for a vending machine breakfast–pastry and spritz of cold water from the bathroom faucet before he had to report to the brig. In the hours before therapy, he hadn't been able to accomplish much besides staring at his feet and focusing on not vomiting. Neither were particularly helpful to his investigation.

On the good news side, Brynn wasn't at therapy. It wasn't often that Dixie was happy to avoid the company of the fairer sex and especially when that fairer sex was also willing to talk to him, but he was still hung over, wearing a child's shirt, and covered in glue, and he didn't feel that his current state was an accurate representation of his sexual appeal.

Dixie walked around the gymnasium and across a worn dirt path toward the main road. It wasn't the most direct route back to the front office, but he needed a little more fresh air before he could endure the discount perfume and keyboard clicks wafting over from the secretarial pool into the brig.

He ducked under the metal railing, followed the zigzag of the concrete path to the main road, and stopped.

"How was therapy?"

Brynn leaned against a Volkswagen and alternated between cigarette puffs and sips off a jumbo soda cup.

"Uhh . . . pretty good." Dixie reached up to smooth down his cowlick and inflate his chest before he stepped onto the sidewalk.

"You look like crap."

"Yeah . . . last night was kinda rough" Dixie released the accumulated wind from his chest cavity and walked to the Volkswagen. "I met your boyfriend."

"Really? How'd that go?"

"Uhh . . . we had a nice conversation," Dixie said, and moved his hand to shade the glare off the car's windshield. "So, it turns out he's not so much a meth dealer as a Christian."

"Yeah . . . I guess he was just trying to impress me."
Brynn sucked back a long slurp on her soda. "They got a
pretty good sale on Sudafed down at Davos's pharmacy, if
you wanted to cook your own. . . . Try not to blow up your
garage, though."

"Check."

Sudafed . . . Sudafed . . . Of course! Cold medicine was
one of the main ingredients in meth production. That was
brilliant! The cartel couldn't make any meth without cold
medicine, and Davos's was the only pharmacy in town. He
just needed to get his hands on their sales records, and they
would lead him straight to the kingpin.

Dixie looked at Brynn and smiled. She really had a good
mind for this kind of work. Not to mention a sweet rack.
Both were good for their long-term romantic prospects.

"Well, see you around, then." Brynn dropped her cigarette onto the ground and turned to walk away.

"Wait . . ." Dixie didn't know how to finish, but he
wanted to end their time together on a high note. "You're . . .
uh . . . I missed you in therapy today."

That wasn't quite it.

Brynn stopped and turned back. "Really?"

"Yeah, uhh . . . so do you maybe want to get together
some time and meditate?"

It might not have been the best idea for a first date, but
that was the only common interest Dixie could think of, and
according to the *Redbook* his mom kept in the bathroom,
that was important.

Brynn smiled. "Freaking weird, dude."

"So, is that a yes?"

Brynn reached out and brushed a strand of loose hair out of Dixie's eyes. He felt a shudder run through his body, a tingle in his thighs, and a burning sensation behind his eyeballs. It was a beautiful moment, something straight from a romance movie. Well, except for the boner, but Dixie figured that was probably why they never panned down in *The Notebook*.

Dixie closed his eyes and leaned into her hand. There were still complications to their relationship—meth-dealing ex-boyfriend, Hepatitis C contracted from meth-dealing ex-boyfriend, knife wounds from jealous, meth-dealing ex-boyfriend, etc.—but Dixie wasn't worried about all that. He just wanted to enjoy the moment, because he knew that it couldn't get any more perfect.

He was right.

A car honked and Dixie turned toward the noise.

It got worse.

"Hey, pixie dick!"

Much, much worse.

Rick angled his dusty, red pickup off the main road and double-parked next to the sidewalk. The albino sat in the passenger seat, and Funt was somehow crammed into the backseat.

Funt leaned across the albino and stuck his head out the window. "Nice shirt, douche bag!"

Dixie turned back to Brynn. "Uhh . . . try to ignore them."

She didn't respond but kept staring at the truck, pale and tense.

Dixie leaned in to tell her that they were actually pretty harmless unless they were naked in the locker room, but something extraordinary happened first.

"Holy crap," the albino said. "Is that Brynn?"

No, extraordinary wasn't quite the right word. More like horrific.

"Damn, girl, you gotta stop following me." Rick stretched across the truck and tossed a soda cup out the window. "I'll get to ya when I get to ya."

Horrific. Definitely. Horrific.

The cup bounced off the asphalt and settled at Dixie's feet. It was from the same convenience store as the cup in Brynn's hands. He supposed that made sense; it was the closest store to the school and the best place in town to score jo jo potatoes.

"Okay, okay, I guess I'll let you take another ride," Rick said, and blew a kiss toward Brynn. "Just like old times."

That one was a bit more difficult for Dixie to explain.

"Do you know him?" Dixie asked Brynn, but she had already turned and sprinted toward campus.

Unfortunately, that's where Dixie was standing.

The impact sent Dixie spinning onto the sidewalk, and Brynn's soda toppled over and spilled on his head.

"Damn!" The albino hooted and slapped the dashboard. "She just beasted that kid."

Dixie wiped the ice cubes and Mountain Dew off his face and watched Brynn hurry past the gymnasium and disappear around the corner. They didn't cover this in the *Redbook* article.

"Oh, sorry about that," Rick said. "I didn't mean to make your girlfriend run away."

Dixie clenched his fist and turned to the truck. "She's not my girlfriend."

"Yeah, you don't love them hos, right?" Rick laughed and pounded fists with the albino. "Old pixie dick's a real skank magnet, ain't he?"

"She's not a skank, you asshole!"

They didn't hear him. They had already driven away in a cloud of dust, laughter, and Top 40 R & B. And besides, Dixie had only shouted it in his mind.

Rick's truck turned the corner, and Dixie felt his skin burn where his fingernails had dug red, angry trenches into his palm. No, they didn't hear him this time, but by the time he was through with those assholes, they'd be the ones who were called skanks, right after some guy in juvie bought them for a pair of socks and a cheese sandwich. He was going to make them pay.

Dixie took out his notebook and flipped to the Six W page.

And he knew just where to start:

HOW: Meth kingpin cooked meth for
     football team using cold medicine
     from local pharmacy?

It was a long shot, sure, but this was the strongest lead he had, and just as soon as he dropped in on the pharmacy and charmed his way into some sales records, he would finally have enough evidence to track down the kingpin and destroy his cartel.

Dixie flipped his notebook shut, pushed up to his feet, and walked through campus to the "Tower."

The pharmacy was on the other side of town, and he was in no condition for that long of a jog. He needed a ride, and lucky for him, this was Ms. Trasker's free period.

Dixie walked across the hall to Ms. Trasker's classroom, paused to brush his sugar-encrusted hair to the side, and decided that perhaps "lucky" wasn't quite the right word to describe the situation.

He pushed open the door and walked inside. Ms. Trasker sat at her desk in the back of the room, reading a celebrity gossip magazine.

"I need another favor," Dixie said.

Ms. Trasker licked her finger and flipped to the next page of the magazine. "You know better than to disturb me while I'm preparing for my next class."

"I know." She was currently teaching the Middle Eastern segment of her world history class. Dixie imagined that watching *Aladdin* for the fifty-eighth time had to be quite spiritually taxing. "But this is important."

"Fine." Ms. Trasker sighed and tossed the magazine onto her desk. "What's with the shirt?"

"It's kind of a long story," Dixie said. "Look, I need you to drive me to the pharmacy. That's the favor."

"Why?"

Dixie shuffled his feet and stared down at Ms. Trasker's reasonably priced pumps. "Do you want the answer where

I lie to you or the answer where I tell you about my investigation."

"You better lie to me."

"I need prophylactics."

"Not that big a lie, Dixie." Ms. Trasker stared at the clock above the door and nodded. "It's gonna cost ya."

Dixie expected that. Nobody could chisel a favor off Ms. Trasker without selling off a little piece of their soul— but this was more important than personal liberty or self-respect.

"Anything."

This was revenge.

Chapter 17

Ms. Trasker pulled her Mazda to the pharmacy's curb and jacked up the parking brake. "You have five minutes."

Dixie nodded. She had fulfilled her part of the agreement. Dixie's end of the bargain was slightly steeper (one Kit Kat from the vending machine, one corsage for her dress at the dance, one year of copyediting the *Wildcat* after graduation), but the price was worth it. The sales records at the pharmacy were a crucial lead, and he was running out of time to piece his investigation together.

Ms. Trasker rolled down her window and pushed in the cigarette lighter on her dash.

"Off the wagon again, ma'am?" Dixie asked. The look she shot back was yet another reminder that such comments were best left for the privacy of internal monologue and his blog. "Right, five minutes."

Dixie stepped out of the car and jogged across the parking lot and up the worn brick path to the wood paneled building. It was a popular destination. The pharmacy was located in perfect triangulation with the hospital, elementary school, and nursing home—the ideal location to serve the varying medical, social, and SweeTart needs of the community.

He pushed open the glass door and stepped inside. A small bell and Eastern European grumbling announced his entrance.

The Eastern European was Mr. Davos, the proud owner and operator of the pharmacy, who excelled in the business despite one slight deficiency in customer service: a complete hatred of all humanity.

"How many are you? Only two child in store at one time!"

Well, maybe not all humanity, just the ones born after 1973.

Mr. Davos stood behind an elevated counter in the back of the room. A small radio on top of his computer played classical music. Behind him an open door led to the storage room.

"Good afternoon, sir," Dixie said.

"Don't steal!" Mr. Davos slapped the counter and the coins in the penny cup flipped onto their sides. "I'm watching you!"

"Sure thing." The malice was real enough, but Davos was bluffing on the "watching you" part. His eyes were too milky to be good for much besides scowling, and though he kept a pair of thick spectacles dangling off a chain on his neck, he never used them. Mr. Davos tracked customers by smelling their fear.

Dixie scanned through the rows of cane tips and chewing gum until he found the display of Sudafed, and at $5.99 a bottle, what budget-conscious meth dealer could resist such a bargain. He grabbed a bottle and walked to the counter.

"Excuse me?"

Mr. Davos lifted his eyes from the computer and drilled lasers into Dixie's forehead. "What?"

Dixie set the cold medicine on the counter. "Do you sell much of this?"

"What are you wearing?" Davos squinted at Dixie and scowled. "That shirt is too tight for you."

"I'm experiencing a growth spurt." Dixie pushed the bottle closer to Davos. "So, does this stuff work?"

"Sure, sure . . . good for sniffle." Davos grabbed his barcode reader and waved the red light over the side of the box until the computer beeped. "Six thirty eight."

"Great . . . but, I guess I still have a few questions."

Mr. Davos leaned over the counter, and his spectacles collided against the register. "What?"

Dixie smiled; it was time to turn up the charm. "Like, I was wondering if . . . you know, maybe I could talk to somebody who's bought this before. See how they liked it, that sorta thing."

Mr. Davos frowned. "No."

"It's no big deal," Dixie said. "Maybe just print me out a copy of your sales records for the last few months, and I'll contact them myself. It won't be any trouble."

Mr. Davos gritted his teeth and reholstered the barcode reader. "Get out."

"What? I'm just trying to be an informed consumer."

"No! I don't need tight-shirt boys talking crazy and wasting my time." Mr. Davos pointed past Dixie's ear to the exit. "Either buy or go."

Dixie sighed; so much for the charm approach. That left just one solution to this situation: outmaneuvering his opponent with superior intellect.

"Okay, okay . . ." Dixie looked past Mr. Davos to the open door into the back. "What I really need is the morning-after pill."

"What? You are girl?" Mr. Davos lifted his glasses and studied Dixie through the magnification. "No, you are not girl . . . are you?"

"No, I'm not a girl."

"So you had unprotected sex with girl?"

Dixie nodded and suppressed the urge to reach across the counter for a high five; this was the closest he'd ever come to losing his virginity.

Mr. Davos shook his head. "No. I don't believe it."

"Why not?"

"You're bony and weak. Very unattractive." Mr. Davos slid his glasses off his nose and coughed. "No. No girl would want you."

Dixie cringed; he didn't expect that that would hurt his feelings so much coming from an elderly Yugoslavian. It was probably time to start increasing his push-up regimen. "Just get me the pills, okay?"

"Are you homoseshual?" Mr. Davos asked. "You know, boy cannot get pregnant by other boy."

"No, I'm not. . . . Look, if I ask for the morning-after pill, you have to give it to me," Dixie said. "It's a state law."

Well, at least Dixie hoped it was. He distinctly remembered hearing something about that on the news while flipping through the channels for insect documentaries and cleavage shots.

"Fine . . . fine." Mr. Davos walked through the door into the storeroom, mumbling "decadence," and "homoseshual," until he turned the corner and disappeared out of earshot.

It was time to move.

Dixie scanned the room for surveillance cameras or lingering customers, found none, lifted his belly onto the edge of the counter, and kicked his legs over into a smooth ninja somersault onto the other side.

Well, that was the plan, at least. The execution of the thing proved a bit more problematic. But besides kicking the penny cup off the counter, and crashing into a display of calcium supplements, the maneuver worked about as well as he expected.

"What's going on out there?" Mr. Davos yelled from the back room. "Don't steal!"

Dixie disentangled himself from the display, pushed the storeroom door shut, and wedged a floor-model cane between the handle and the floor.

"Hey!" The door bulged from the inside and Dixie jumped back. "What are you doing? I'll call the police!"

Dixie stared at the door until he was sure that the barricade would hold, then turned to the computer. He had to work fast; Mr. Davos didn't have the bone density to break down the door, but he probably kept a phone back there, so the police threat was real enough.

"Let me out!" Davos shouted, and banged on the inside of the door. "You let me out, homoseshual boy!"

Dixie twisted up the volume on the radio to drown out Davos and turned to the computer. The screen was filled with a chart of yellow-on-black text about the Sudafed. He clicked the mouse on the SALES HISTORY icon on the bottom of the page, and the screen blinked into columns of dates, quantities, and credit card information.

He scanned through the list of last month's purchases and stopped. "Holy crap!"

```
CREDIT CARD HOLDER          AMOUNT        DATE
Ralphino, D                 100 units     9/2/08
```

Dixie looped the cursor around the last name and reached for his notebook. That was the guy.

WHO: Ralphino is the meth kingpin.

He stared at the entry for a moment and then dotted the *i* in Ralphino's name with a smiley face. It wasn't the most professional move, but Dixie felt like he'd earned the celebration. He had finally found the meth kingpin! The purchase date even coincided with the start of football season, and once he did a little more digging, Dixie was pretty sure that he'd find some overdoses around that time, as well.

Dixie snapped his notebook shut and smiled. His

investigation was finally starting to come together. Nothing could stop him now—

"Where's Mr. Davos?"

—Except, maybe that.

Dixie looked down: a chubby kid with a cowlick and a strand of Red Vines in his fist stared up at the counter. Evidently, the lower grades had been excused from the elementary school.

"I'm his nephew," Dixie said, and lowered his face behind the cover of the cash register. He suspected that the kid had much more reliable vision than Mr. Davos.

"Hey! Let me out!" Mr. Davos shouted over the Mozart and banged against the door. "I will put you in choke hold!"

The kid leaned over the counter and looked toward the ruckus. "Is that Mr. Davos?"

"Uhh . . . yeah." Dixie turned back to the door and coughed. "I put him on a time-out. . . . He was using swear words."

"Oh . . ." The kid said, and shifted his focus to Dixie. "Will you teach me kung fu?"

"I'm not Chinese."

Dixie heard a squeak at the front of the store and looked at the noise. A crowd of children bunched at the door, tracing their dirty fingers against the glass, and staring at the shelves of processed sugar.

"Can you throw a fireball?" the kid asked. "I promise I won't tell."

Dixie stared at the display of Lion Mints on the counter and smiled.

"Hey, tell you what . . ." Dixie grabbed a handful of mints off the counter and handed them to the kid. "These are free."

"Really?"

"Yeah . . . so's that Red Vine." Dixie waved in the kids from their holding pattern at the front door. "All the candy's free, today! Tell your friends!"

The kids streamed into the store and knocked over a rack of Metamucil to get to the candy.

Dixie took one last look at the computer screen, grabbed a package of Lion Mints, and rolled over onto the ground level. More children rushed inside. Dixie dodged the stream of miniature looters and walked to the front of the store. It would take hours for the police to sort through this chaos, and by the time they sent out an APB for a "bony, homoseshual tight-shirt boy," he would be miles away. It was the perfect crime.

He stopped at the door and noticed a cardboard poster taped to the glass:

Spaghetti Feed Fund-Raiser
for Stilton High Football

7 pm at Stilton High Cafeteria

Silent Auction to Follow

Dixie peeled the poster off the glass and folded it into his pocket. He had the name for the kingpin but nowhere near enough time to track down his identity. That was okay, though; he could always just let the meth kingpin come to him. The game was only twenty-four hours away; the candy man would have to make his delivery before too long, and Dixie would be ready with his camera just as soon as that happened. Also, an apron and, possibly, a hairnet; he was about to go undercover in the food service industry.

He pushed open the pharmacy door, jogged across the parking lot, and plunked down inside Ms. Trasker's car. "Got it."

Ms. Trasker flicked the end of her cigarette out the window and clicked the gear shifter to D. "What's with all the kids?"

"Uhh . . . they were having a sale on Pokemon cards."

"Really?"

Dixie shrugged. "They're collectibles."

Ms. Trasker backed her car out of the pharmacy's parking lot and rolled on to the main road. "Goddamn Japanese pop culture is ruining this country."

Dixie watched the pharmacy disappear into the distance in the rearview mirror, unwrapped a mint off the roll in his pocket, and crunched down on the chalky disk. The spaghetti feed was just a few hours away, and he needed to be in top form for his undercover operation.

Speaking of top form . . .

"I'll dance with you for a slow song if you run by my house for a quick change of clothes," Dixie said.

"Two slow songs and no erections."

"Deal."

Chapter 18

Thursday, 7:36 p.m.

The Stilton community ignored the local theater, avoided all restaurants that didn't prominently feature flapjacks and American cheese, and ranged from apathetic to hostile toward all sports not football or basketball. Despite these selective and refined tastes, there was still one universally supported event in the county: charity spaghetti feeds.

In the last month, Dixie had attended spaghetti feed benefits for the 4-H, some kid with leukemia, the Sheriff's Posse, and the Boy Scouts. And though there were enough vowels in the county's surnames to expect some top shelf pasta, the quality of the food ranged from awful, to clumpy and awful.

Still, Dixie was excited. Tonight, he was working undercover on the food preparation line to spy on the football team. Plus, he got an unlimited supply of garlic bread. There were a variety of factors.

So far, the operation had gone remarkably smooth.

The organizers had accepted Dixie as a volunteer without too many questions and suited him up with a hairnet and apron within ten minutes of entering the cafeteria.

Out of respect to the sergeant (currently a garlic bread assistant and proud member of the organization) the good members of the Elks or Moose (Dixie wasn't really paying attention—definitely something with a hoof) had skipped Dixie ahead of the rookie's usual dishwashing responsibilities and put him to work mixing orange juice in the kitchen.

Dixie appreciated the special treatment: the sanitary gloves protected him from leaving any fingerprints, the stirring was good for muscle tone, and from the kitchen window he had a clear view of the football players' table.

He poured a pitcher of water into the barrel of orange juice concentrate, stirred the slush with a long wooden spatula, and stared at the jocks in the center of the cafeteria. That's right, druggies, eat your garlic bread, Dixie thought; little did they know a trained professional was monitoring their every move.

Unfortunately, beyond a series of sharp pains in his lower back when he lifted the barrel of juice concentrate, the night had been fairly anticlimactic. There were no drug deals, or meth injections, and the football players were too busy eating their weight in steaming carbs to do anything illegal. Evidently, heart disease got them in "game spirit."

A familiar mustache in an unfamiliar yellow apron stuck his head through the open door of the kitchen. "Hurry up on that OJ, Dixie!"

Dixie nodded at his father. "Right away, sir."

The sergeant pulled his head out of the kitchen, and

Dixie followed his progress across the cafeteria and back to the garlic bread station. He supposed this was probably why most investigative reporters didn't go on undercover assignments with their immediate family.

Dixie grabbed the spatula and stirred the slush until the congealed block of syrup sank beneath the surface, then looked back to the football players' table.

"Oh crap!" Somewhere between getting yelled at by the sergeant and stirring the orange juice, the albino had sat down next to Funt.

This was bad. Very bad. They could have already completed the drug handoff, and even if they hadn't, he didn't have a clear angle to see under the table. He needed to get closer.

Dixie looked down at the slow revolution of the spatula around the vortex of orange juice; this called for something drastic.

He bent down as low as the snugness of his jeans allowed, clamped his forearms against the sides of the juice barrel, and thrust it up and into the sink.

After a whole lot of hope, and just a bit more water pressure, he forced the chunks of ice and juice down the drain.

He tucked the empty juice barrel underneath his arm and walked out of the kitchen to the fruit-salad preparation line. "I need more juice mix."

A white haired banana slicer at the end of the table looked up at Dixie. "You're out?"

"Yeah . . ." Dixie lifted up the empty barrel. "I guess they're pretty thirsty tonight."

She raised her eyebrow and pointed her knife at the barrel. "That was supposed to make twenty gallons."

Dixie dropped his eyes and stepped back. He made it a general rule to limit conversation with aggravated people holding sharp objects.

The banana slicer continued to stare at him, trying to decide whether he was lying or just stupid. Dixie figured it was best to nudge her toward the latter. "I wasn't supposed to mix in water with it, was I?"

She sighed and waved her knife toward the back of the cafeteria. A chunk of banana whistled off the blade and stuck against Dixie's forehead. "There's some more in the freezer."

Dixie wiped off the debris. "Thanks."

"And young man, try to read the directions this time." She reached another banana out of a cardboard box and slit down the peel. "We're trying to raise money for the football team, not subsidize Florida's economy."

Dixie nodded and walked away. This episode wouldn't reflect too well on his father. They might even demote him to salad tosser for this, and the title of the position alone was demeaning for a man of the law, but Dixie had bigger concerns than his father's humiliation or wasted juice. He was just a few feet from his targets and about to crack his investigation.

He walked across the cafeteria and dipped down toward the football player's table. Such a direct penetration of enemy territory was a dangerous move, but so long as he maintained a constant speed, kept his ears perked, and covered his face with the juice barrel, Dixie was sure he'd be fine.

Unfortunately, the walking proved a bit problematic.

As soon as Dixie arrived within earshot of the football table, his cross trainer found an apple slice where it expected linoleum and initiated a chain of events that started with a yip and ended with a groan, with an awkward tumble somewhere in between.

"You okay?" a familiar gruff voice called from the back of the room.

Dixie looked back to see the sergeant holding a loaf of greasy bread in one hand and a paintbrush full of butter in the other. "Fine," he said.

Dixie hadn't heard the sergeant that concerned since the inevitable conclusion of his turn on the pony ride at the 1998 state fair. That turned out well enough in the end, though. Dixie wasn't using his clavicle that much, anyway.

"Get up then." The sergeant turned back to the table. A dollop of yellow liquid dripped off the end of his paintbrush onto the floor.

Dixie nodded and lifted a thumbs-up to his father. He was glad to see the sergeant resume his standard emotional cycle of embarrassment, confusion, and anger. Things were starting to get a little weird there for a moment.

He heard a series of muffled giggles and turned to the noise. The football players stared back, and Dixie was sure that the giggles would have escalated to full-blown laughter and light torture, if not for a mutual fear of his father. His cover was blown.

Dixie grabbed the juice barrel off the ground and walked to the back freezer. He wasn't ready to give up, yet.

He would pass by the football players' table again on his return trip with the new barrel of frozen orange juice, and that left him one more chance for reconnaissance—

He opened the door to the back freezer, walked past the frozen hash-brown squares and nacho-cheese drums to the juice barrels, and power squatted the closest off the rack.

—Just with much more heavy lifting this time.

Dixie waddled out of the room and started the long trudge across the cafeteria back to the football players' table. The barrel was heavy and cold, and Dixie wanted to stop, but Magnus Ver Magnusson, four-time winner of the World's Strongest Man competition (and Iceland's proudest export since herring and discordant pop music) never quit, and he wouldn't either.

He stepped forward. One foot after the other. Eyes on the ground. Strain to the back.

It wasn't so bad, almost relaxing. Maybe a career in manual labor wouldn't be so bad, after all. His dad had connections down at the limestone mine. That was a growth profession.

"So, you get some yet?"

Wear a hard hat. Shovel some rock. Have a cold one with the fellas after work.

"Not quite."

"What do you mean, not quite?"

Meet a pretty little girl at the honky tonk bar. Settle down. Buy a truck.

"Just like I said it."

"You pussed out, didn't you?"

Join the Elks. Stir some noodles with his dad. Wear a funny hat.

"No, I'm just waiting for the right moment is all."

"She's a slut, Funt. . . . Just grab her and do your thing."

Dixie looked up from his sneakers. He was standing next to Funt and the albino at the football players' table. With all the strain on his lower back, he'd almost forgotten that he was on assignment.

"That's rape, dude."

"Well, don't jump out from behind a tree or whatever, but, you know, the basics."

Dixie shifted his weight from one foot to the other to approximate walking and leaned in closer to their conversation.

"You can't ejaculate the night before a game, man. It takes your legs."

"Funt, you scratch your nuts on the sideline and pass out Gatorade. A cripple could do that."

"Nah, I'm starting. Steve's sick."

The barrel slipped down Dixie's forearms, and he arched back to support the weight against his thighs. It hurt, but there was no time like the present to cultivate a lifetime of joint pain.

"Still?"

"Yeah."

"Man, that's some tainted shit going around."

Dixie stepped closer. Tainted shit? What did that mean? Bad meth? Football players were getting sick from bad meth? That meant hospital treatments, medical bills, insurance forms, prescriptions. . . . There had to be some kind of paper trail connecting all this back to Ralphino and the football team.

This was big; even better than a drug handoff. He needed to get his hands on the football team's medical records, and he could tie the rest of it together. This was just the break he was looking for. This—

Someone gripped Dixie's shoulder before his plan could crystallize.

"Hey there, pixie dick."

He turned. It was Rick. Usually that meant bad things for Dixie.

But, apparently, Rick hadn't watched too many episodes of the "World's Strongest Man." Otherwise, he would have known the dangers of startling a power lifter during competition. Especially when that someone is only an amateur in the sport, and the startler is wearing sandals.

Chapter 19

Thursday, 9:06 p.m.

After the ambulance left, things got a lot quieter at the spaghetti feed. And though nobody said the exact words to Dixie (in fact, nobody said much besides "jackass" and "moron"), he figured it was probably best for him to leave.

Dixie stepped outside, dashed up the steps to the quad, and ducked for cover behind a trash can.

"Holy crap."

He had just broken Rick Johnson's foot. Rick Johnson. The biggest force of malevolence and terror in Dixie's life since the third grade, and he had just rearranged his metatarsals with a barrel of frozen orange juice.

Dixie gulped hard and squeezed his arms against his thighs to settle the quakes in his hands. That's strange—for the amount of time he had spent fantasizing about this kind of scenario, he had always expected it would feel a lot more satisfying. Of course, it's difficult to fully appreciate the consequences of cause and effect while daydreaming in church.

Rick was going to be pissed. No, that didn't quite capture it—Rick was going to kill him.

He already gave Dixie wedgies and dunked him in the toilet, and that was just to punish him for existing. But what now? This had to be worse than existing, at least ten times worse, and though Dixie wasn't exactly sure what a wedgie to the tenth power entailed, he was fairly certain that he wouldn't enjoy it.

This was bad.

Dixie patted the ground for potential weapons and checked the cafeteria's back door to make sure he wasn't being tailed.

His investigation had officially taken a turn for the deadly in the last few minutes. Still, Dixie wasn't ready to give up. Not when he was so close to breaking this story and proving his innocence. Sure, Rick wanted to kill him, and continued surveillance of the football team was going to be difficult and painful (mostly painful) after the incident in the cafeteria, but now that he knew about the "tainted shit," he didn't need to waste his time on covert surveillance, anyway. The key to his investigation was the football players recuperating in a series of extra large recumbent beds down at the hospital. Just as soon as Dixie got a hold of their medical records, he would finally have enough evidence to take down Ralphino's cartel.

Dixie smiled; he'd be safe once he sent Rick and the rest of the football team to juvenile hall. Well, at least until they were paroled and set out looking for revenge, but that wouldn't be for another ten years. Hopefully that would leave him enough time to win a Pulitzer and lose his virginity, which seemed like a pretty full life.

He peeked over the top of the trash can to scout for any wandering lynch mobs or parental units but found none. He supposed that made sense; the football players were still too sluggish with carbohydrates to pose much of an immediate threat, and the sergeant was far too embarrassed and angry to even acknowledge his son's existence, let alone remember that he was supposed to drive him home after the dinner.

Dixie leaned back against the trash can, closed his eyes, and tried to figure out his next move.

He envisioned two options:

1. Jog down to hospital. Seduce candy striper. Steal candy striper's uniform while she is sleeping. Sneak into hospital. Hack into computer system. Take football player's medical files.

2. Well, this was one was pretty much identical to number one, but instead of hacking into the computer, he would beat a confession out of one of the football players with a bedpan.

Dixie peeled the hairnet off his scalp and tossed it into the trash can. Perhaps those plans were a bit extreme. Besides, he didn't want to abandon his surveillance of the football team and spend the rest of the night sneaking around the hospital and abusing meth-sick jocks just to find out this was some kind of seasonal sniffle.

No, he needed something more concrete than idle gossip, some solid proof that this lead was more than just wild speculation—

Dixie looked across the empty quad to the front office and smiled.

—And he knew just where to find it.

The school kept their attendance records in there. All that left was jimmying a lock and flipping through some file cabinets, and he could still make it back home in time for a bowl of Crispix and a *Becker* rerun. It was the perfect solution.

He stalked across the quad to the office's back door, twisted the handle, pushed on the wood, scraped his student ID against the dead bolt, and decided that breaking into the building would require a bit more than just the desire to do so.

That was disappointing. It always looked so easy in the movies, and that was with the added obstacles of security robots, ninjas, or security robot ninjas, if the film was particularly well made.

Dixie backed up a few steps and aimed his shoulder at the door. He was hoping it wouldn't come to this, but figured that it worked too well for Magnum P.I. to not give it a shot.

And of course, Tom Selleck wasn't built like Natalie Portman. That was probably crucial to the success of the maneuver.

He bounced off the wood and crumpled to the ground. The door wasn't broken. Neither was his shoulder. Dixie was willing to call it a draw.

"What are you doing?"

Dixie tensed. The security ninjas had found him, and they sounded cute. Well, this was awkward.

"I'm having a seizure!" Dixie rolled onto his back and churned his legs in the air. "Find a doctor!"

"No you're not, Dixie. Jesus."

He stopped kicking his legs and looked up. It was Brynn. That's funny; she didn't look like a ninja. "Howdy."

"What are you doing?"

Dixie rolled onto his stomach and pushed up to his feet. "It's complicated."

"Really?"

"Yeah . . ." Dixie wiped the dirt and loose pebbles off his shirt. "Kinda top secret."

Brynn smiled. "Top secret like you breaking Rick's foot? Or is that not complicated enough."

Wow, the rumor mill churned much faster than Dixie expected.

"Uhh . . . that was more of an accident."

"That's not what I saw."

"You were there?"

Brynn shrugged. "I like the noodles."

"Oh." The culinary scene in Stilton was in a much more desperate condition than Dixie remembered. It was probably high time for the town to open a second Applebee's.

"So, you gonna break down that door, or what?" Brynn asked.

Dixie rubbed his shoulder. "Yeah . . . I was just warming up."

Brynn reached down the neck of her shirt and fished out something small and metal, and for the first time in his life,

Dixie wished that he were something small and metal. "Why don't you just use the key?"

No. Freaking. Way.

She walked to the door, stuck the key in the lock, and pushed it open.

"How did you get that?" Dixie asked.

"It's complicated." Brynn smiled and walked inside the building.

Dixie watched her disappear around the corner, then followed.

"So, what are we looking for?" Brynn asked after Dixie closed the door.

We. Dixie liked the sound of that. He looked down at the fingertips extending from the sleeves of her black sweatshirt and contemplated reaching for her hand. He was pretty sure couples progressed to that after shared pronouns, followed eventually by intercourse and monogrammed towels.

He stuck his hands back into his pockets. It was probably best to hold off on any romantic advances until they were finished breaking and entering.

"Student records," Dixie said. "I need a list of all medical absences from varsity PE for the last few weeks."

He didn't expect that sort of thing would be too difficult to find—just open the file cabinet in the center of the room and flip through the manila envelopes. Unfortunately, the school owned more than just one cabinet (they probably found filing was much easier that way), and the drawers were labeled with abbreviations that Dixie couldn't decipher.

He walked to a tall cabinet in the center of the room and grabbed the top handle; random selection was just about as effective as anything else he could think of at the moment.

He pulled back on the drawer. And continued to pull. "No way!"

"What?" Brynn walked over and stood next to Dixie.

"It's locked." Dixie turned back to face her. "You don't have a key for that, too, do you?'

"Sure." Brynn picked a three-hole punch off the desk and pounded against the drawer until something popped, and the drawer rolled open.

Dixie took his hands away from his face. "That works." Brynn needed a little instruction on the finer points of covert reconnaissance (massive property damage tended to draw unwanted attention), but still, he admired her gumption.

Dixie thumbed into the guts of the drawer, pulled out a fistful of folders, and laid them across the desk for easy viewing.

"Dang." It wasn't quite what he wanted. In fact, Dixie couldn't imagine anyone ever having much use for the 1993 school bus oil-change records, but then again, large diesel engines weren't really his area of expertise.

He dropped his forehead onto the files; there wasn't enough time or blunt objects to go through all these cabinets tonight. He was screwed.

Brynn picked up a candy bowl off the nearest desk and busied herself with licking the Skittles. "You find it?"

"No . . . this is pointless."

"Why don't you just try the computer?"

Dixie lifted his head from the files. That was brilliant. He was sure that the secretaries had figured out those electronic boxes on their desks could be used for something besides showcasing pictures of their grandchildren.

He grabbed a mostly dry candy from the bowl and looked up at Brynn. "So . . . do you know much about that sorta thing?"

As it turned out, Brynn knew quite a bit about computers. And though it was a shot to Dixie's intellectual pride to find someone more proficient with the machine, and damaging to his masculine confidence that this particular someone also happened to squat during urination, he didn't let it keep him down.

Besides, she wasn't better at everything, just hacking into protected systems and scouring hard drives. Let's see her stalk out free porn on a 56k dialup; let's just see how smart she looks then.

Dixie pushed off with his feet and rolled his office chair back into a filing cabinet. He realized that his actions may appear as sulking to the untrained observer, but he was actually in the midst of searching for clues. Backward. In an office chair. The sulking bit was just a comforting by-product.

"How's it going?" Dixie asked.

"Good," Brynn said. "You want me to change any grades for you?'

"No thanks."

"Hey, what's with the nervous diarrhea thing in your medical file?"

"Focus, Brynn!"

Of course, it was probably for the best that she found out about that now. Dixie would hate to explain that one on their wedding night.

Dixie flexed his legs off the filing cabinet and crashed back hard into a desk. A little too hard: a vase of flowers tipped into his lap, and something metal clanged down onto the carpet.

"Blast!" Dixie jumped out of the chair and wiped the water and rose petals off his lap.

"You okay?" Brynn asked, but kept her eyes fixed on the computer screen.

"Uhh . . . yeah. Just a charley horse."

Upon further reflection, Dixie decided that he probably shouldn't have lied about that. The crotch dampness was going to be difficult to explain the next time they got under adequate lighting.

Dixie scanned the room for something to absorb the water on his pants and grabbed a handful of white paper slips from the open lid of the box that knocked onto the ground. He patted the papers against his crotch. Blue ink stained through the paper and onto his hand.

He lifted the damp, blue pulp next to his face, and looked closer. There was something written on those papers, and Dixie decided that he'd probably go a lot further in this world if he took a moment to examine things before he rubbed them against his crotch.

Dixie grabbed the metal box off the ground and looked at the label on the side: HOMECOMING KING NOMINATIONS. He picked up another slip of paper and held it up against the faint light from the digital clock on the desk: RICK JOHNSON.

Rick's name was written on the second ballot. And the third. Fourth. Eighteenth. Dixie turned over fifty ballots before he found a differing vote, and even then, he doubted that "crudely drawn vagina" could drum up enough popular support to carry the election.

Dixie gathered the ballots into the box, and dumped them into the trash. He hated to subvert the democratic process, but the students at Stilton High clearly weren't enlightened enough to be trusted with the power of the ballot. Not if they were going to elect that douche bag.

He pulled the pen off his shirt pocket, peeled a slip of paper from the pile on the desk, wrote

BRANDON PRESTO

in block letters, and dropped it into the empty box.

Besides, if anyone deserved to wear a crown for a few minutes, it was Brandon—

Dixie grabbed another paper, wrote

Brandon Presto

in flowing cursive, and dropped it next to the first.

—He'd been having one hell of a difficult week.

After several hundred votes for his brother and three significant hand cramps, Dixie looked up from the ballots and saw Brynn standing in front of his desk.

"You find anything?" Dixie asked.

"Yeah. That lady had a gig of *Cathy* cartoons on her

hard drive." Brynn said. "Oh, and I'm class salutatorian now."

Dixie made a mental note to attend graduation; that was sure to be an interesting speech.

"That's good," Dixie said.

Brynn reached down the front of her shirt and pulled out a packet of cigarettes. Dixie was amazed that she had the extra storage capacity; her brassiere must have had some kind of fanny-pack attachment.

"Take a look at this." She tapped a cigarette out of the box, walked back to the computer, and Dixie followed. He appreciated the break; election fraud was much more labor intensive than he'd anticipated.

Brynn sat down at the secretary's desk and held the pack of cigarettes over her shoulder. "Want one?"

"Sure." He mangled a cigarette out of the pack, dipped the tip into Brynn's lighter, and looked at the screen:

```
MEDICAL ABSENCES FROM VARSITY PE: 10/18-10/25
Jeff Jefferson      1 week        Illness
Steve Rounkst       1 week        Illness
Jose Islaroja       1 week        Illness
Rob Ziegler         1 week        Illness
```

"Is this it?" Brynn asked.

"Yeah." Dixie scanned through the list of names and sucked back on the cigarette. "This is definitely it."

There must have been some quality-control problems with the last batch of meth, or maybe Ralphino poisoned these guys for wearing the wrong brand of jockstrap; Dixie still hadn't worked out all the details. What really mattered was that all these football players got sick from "tainted shit" the same week that three hobos overdosed off bad meth, and once he got his hands on another drug sample, Dixie could prove this was more than just an interesting coincidence.

"Print it," Dixie said. At least that's what he intended to say—but forcing the words past his lips was difficult without any oxygen. He had to breathe, but that would let in more smoke, and judging by the burn in his sinuses from what was curling up and in from the tip of his cigarette, Dixie was fairly certain that that wasn't something he'd enjoy.

The edges of Dixie's world faded to swirls of gray. He was about to pass out, and that couldn't be good on a first date. Something had to be done, and fast—

"Blahh!" Dixie spit out the cigarette and folded over into a fit of alternating gasps and coughs.

—But unfortunately, the path of the "quick" and the path of the "smooth" did not often intersect at the "now."

"First time?" Brynn asked.

"Don't be crazy," Dixie forced out between fast, desperate gasps. "I've just got a touch of consumption, that's all."

Brynn stared at Dixie and smiled. "Wasn't that cured in the 1850s or something?"

Dixie wiped his nose against his sleeve. "Or maybe it's the sniffles. I'm not sure yet."

"The trash can's on fire."

"So, thumbs up to you for finding the files," Dixie said. "That was clutch."

Wait a minute, what was that last bit about a fire?

"The trash can's on fire!" Dixie jumped back to a safe distance and stared at the flames licking out from the rim of the container.

The spectacle was pretty enough, and nobody got hurt, and Dixie was ready to smooth it all out with a joke when something unfortunate happened: the fire sprinklers turned on. They contained the fire easily enough, but unless everything else in the room was designed to function underwater, this was going to be bad.

"Run!" Brynn sprinted out of the room, and Dixie followed behind.

So bad, in fact, that Dixie couldn't think of any good reason to stick around. He already had a pretty good idea how this was going to turn out.

Chapter 20

Dixie imagined it wasn't Brynn's first time running from a crime scene. He appreciated that. Left to his own devices he probably would have spent his wind running circles around the office before collapsing into a fetal position on the sidewalk. So long as Brynn was in front of him, Dixie didn't have to worry about all that. He just followed her sweet sashay to salvation.

She ducked under the fence behind the front office, slid down the dirt embankment, and sloshed into the shallow, muddy creek that ran through the school.

Dixie followed through the fence (with difficulty), down the embankment (with more difficulty), and stepped through the creek toward Brynn's distant splashes.

The water was cold and slimy and undoubtedly infecting his pores with some strain of Legionnaires' disease, but Dixie was pretty sure there would be much worse than wet feet and itchy toes waiting for him at the county jail.

And his name was probably Eric.

Brynn stopped under the curved arch of a pedestrian bridge by the tennis courts. Dixie followed her into the darkness until he was close enough to distinguish her brand of shampoo. Neutrogena T/Gel. So, she suffered from the shame of dry, flaky scalp as well; Dixie was sure that marriages had started on less.

"You got another cigarette?" Dixie asked. Something light and papery shoved against his face, and after some probes, Brynn stuck the cigarette between his lips. "Thanks."

"No prob." Brynn clicked on her lighter and grazed the fire against Dixie's cigarette. "You probably can't burn anything down here, anyway."

Dixie liked to think that she was using a playful tone. "Is that a challenge?"

Brynn clicked on the flame to light her own cigarette. "Try not to suck back so much. It'll help with the coughing."

"Check." Dixie pulled back on the cigarette enough to scald the roof of his mouth but stopped before the gag reflex took over. He still didn't like it, but one hundred million Japanese couldn't be wrong. Except about World War II. Dixie was pretty sure they'd take a mulligan on that one.

"Is that better?" Brynn asked.

"Yeah." Dixie blew up a cloud of burning smoke into his eyes with the word. He assumed that this was why most smokers were the strong, silent type. "Can I ask you a question?"

"Sure."

"Just how in the hell did you get the key to the front office?"

Brynn laughed and flicked the embers off the tip of her cigarette. "My cheerleading coach gave me a key to the office. . . . You know, so I could get my pom-poms out of storage or whatever."

"You're a cheerleader?" Dixie asked. That would explain how she knew Rick, her pleasing figure, and the blond roots in her hair. Of course, this also raised a number of new mysteries, namely, why the hell she was breaking social caste to talk to him. Dixie felt it was best not to question his good fortune on this one.

"I used to be." Brynn's voice cracked, but she covered it with a long drag on her cigarette. "It's a long story. . . . Some other time, okay?"

"Sure." Dixie coughed, but it wasn't just the tanning shop in his lungs; that was a guilt cough. He couldn't keep any secrets from her. Not anymore. Not after all they'd been through. "I'm not really a meth addict."

Brynn smiled. "No shit."

"No" Dixie said. "No shit. I'm an investigative reporter for the *Wildcat*."

"What's that?"

"It's the school newspaper. . . . They don't pass it out until fifth period."

"Oh."

Dixie made a mental note to talk to Ms. Trasker about delivering the papers a few hours earlier; they were neglecting a key stoner demographic.

"So, you're probably gonna stop coming to therapy, then, huh?" Brynn asked.

"Well, I'm pretty sure it's court ordered," Dixie said. "And, you know . . . the company's nice."

Brynn sparked her cigarette, and Dixie was pretty sure he saw the outline of a smile against the faint illumination.

"I'm sorry I lied to you," Dixie said.

"Well . . . keep taking me out to nice places like this, and I might forgive you."

"Okay." Dixie hoped that the Biblical themed miniature golf course by the library counted as a "nice place." He didn't have much flexibility in his date budget.

A fire engine screamed past the main road, and Dixie and Brynn crouched against the side of the bridge.

"So, do you always set school property on fire, or is this a special occasion?" Brynn asked.

Dixie breathed in until the embers on his cigarette illuminated Brynn's face.

"It's special," Dixie said. "You're special."

He coughed out the column of smoke stashed away in his lungs and thanked God that he spit out the romantic bit before the phlegm.

"Are you flirting with me?"

Dixie wasn't sure. It was the most he'd ever spoken to a woman that wasn't obligated by family relation or paycheck, but it felt right.

"Yes." He stepped forward until the smoke from Brynn's cigarette mingled with his own on a shared journey to his eyes. He didn't mind the blindness. So long as she kept using such an aromatic shampoo, there was no reason their relationship couldn't work. "I think you're a very handsome lady."

The embers on Brynn's cigarette sparked. She was smiling. He took that as a good sign. "Freakin' weird, dude."

He dropped his cigarette into the creek. This was the moment, and he didn't want to spoil the romance by burning her face.

Dixie puckered his lips, leaned forward, and aimed for the beacon of her cigarette. He wasn't sure if this was the right move, or if he was moving too fast, and maybe it was just the adrenaline and nicotine, but Dixie didn't care about all that.

This was what he had to do.

His lips bumped against something fleshy, and Dixie pulled back. He hoped that he made contact with her lips. Their first kiss wouldn't be quite so romantic if he landed it on her shoulder.

"What was that?" Brynn asked.

"I slipped?"

"Jesus Christ, Dixie."

Brynn pulled Dixie against her body, jammed her lips against his face, and slithered her tongue through his teeth, exploring down toward where his tonsils used to dangle.

So, that's how kissing works. Dixie expected less saliva.

He contemplated joining in on the action with a few tongue flicks of his own but decided it was best to take things slow. He didn't want Brynn to think he was a slut.

Dixie wasn't sure how long Brynn stayed in his mouth, but she left far too soon.

"I gotta get going," she said soft and sweet into Dixie's ear. "See you at therapy."

Brynn stuck the remains of her cigarette into Dixie's mouth, and the clomp-splash of her boots was several yards down the creek before he could rally the gray matter to a response.

"Thanks."

Dixie sat down on the cold, slick grass and dragged on the cigarette. He figured it was best to stay put and wait out the arson investigation, then he could walk home and go to bed. He had a big day of stealing meth samples, avoiding jock revenge, and toppling a drug cartel coming up, and he'd need the fortification of a full night's REM cycles to be at his journalistic best.

Chapter 21

Friday, 9:24 a.m.

Dixie wasn't sure if it was the sunlight angling down under the bridge, the ring of the tardy bell, or the stench of the green mold against his check that shook him from his slumber, but they all welcomed him into the new day, and none were so comforting as NPR on his alarm clock radio at home.

As it turned out, arson investigations weren't the quick and breezy affairs that Dixie had anticipated. He wasn't sure when he had come to this conclusion, maybe 1 a.m., maybe 4, but it was definitely sometime before he decided that sleeping in the damp mud and rocks under the bridge might not be so bad, after all.

That was unexpected. Dixie had always thought he was a sensitive sleeper, but as it turned out, he had just never been tired before. Not really.

Dixie walked up the creek's dirt embankment and crossed the street to the school-bus maintenance garage.

Brandon would be working on the float in there, and if the fates were smiling, might even have a few extra dollars to contribute toward Dixie's breakfast.

He pushed open the door to the maintenance garage. A wave of glue fumes surged through the opening and stung his nostrils.

"Brandon?" Dixie plugged his nose, crossed the room to the senior float, and stopped. "Oh sweet Christ!"

Dixie saw a variety of things at that moment: a bowl of yellow, steaming glue, SENIO outlined in colored tissue on the backsplash, a worn pair of jockey underwear hanging off a cardboard cutout of Fred Flintstone. But he was fairly certain that the only thing he'd truly remember was his brother's penis.

Dixie grabbed a pile of plastic flowers off the float and threw them in the general vicinity of his brother's crotch until he was sure that all indecency was sufficiently covered. "Brandon?"

Brandon didn't respond, but Dixie was pretty sure that he was still alive; the heaving chest and erection removed any doubt.

"Brandon!" Dixie grabbed a paint roller off the float and jabbed Brandon in the ribs until he groaned and opened one eye. "Wake up!"

"Huh . . . ? Oh, hey, Dixie." Brandon nestled his head back into a patch of colored tissue and closed his eye. "You look terrible. . . . What happened?"

Dixie looked down at the tracks of mud and moss on his clothes and shrugged. "Oh, just the usual."

"Dad called like three times last night. I told him you were helping me on the float again."

"Thanks."

"Don't mention it." Brandon turned away from the light. "Just let me sleep some more."

"Uhh, Brandon?"

Brandon grunted and turned away. "What?"

"You know you're naked, right?"

"I'm naked?"

"Pretty much."

"Oh?" Brandon opened an eye and looked down his stomach to the morning obelisk. "Yeah . . . I guess me and Julie had sex last night."

"Really?"

"Yeah . . ." Brandon closed his eyes for a moment, and then jackknifed up into a sitting position. "Holy crap!"

"Congratulations!" Dixie reached out for a high five, but Brandon leaned over the side of the float and vomited before they could complete the maneuver.

So, their priest wasn't lying about the pain of premarital sex, after all. Dixie had always assumed that Father Ted was just bitter.

After several heaves, Brandon rolled back onto the float and yanked his underwear off Mr. Flintstone's nose.

"Uhh . . . so, you used protection, right?" Dixie hated to be so indiscreet, but Julie looked like the fertile type, and he felt it was best to establish a damage-control strategy as soon as possible.

Brandon nodded. "Yes . . . no . . . uhh . . . maybe?"

"What?"

"Well, we were working on the float, and then we started talking about music and college or whatever, and then the glue tipped over and . . . oh God!"

Brandon leaned over the side of the float and offered the remainder of yesterday's caloric intake to the asphalt below.

Dixie stepped up onto the float and put his hand on his brother's shoulder. He didn't usually like to touch other men, especially when those other men happened to be naked and vomiting, but this was different. This was family.

"So, you want to get some breakfast or something?" Dixie asked.

Brandon wiped a cord of phlegm off his chin and nodded. "Sure."

Dixie smiled. Sure, times were tough for the Presto brothers. There were pregnancy scares and meth cartels and homecoming floats and grumpy jocks and wilderness-based rehab programs, but at least they had each other—

"You think the snack cart's still open?"

—And Dixie had yet to find a problem that a pack of mini-doughnuts and a cup of coffee couldn't solve.

Chapter 22

Friday, 10:16 a.m.

Dixie stuffed the remaining crescent of mini-doughnut into his mouth and opened the door to the *Wildcat* office. The breakfast had made him feel much better. His head still ached, and algae was colonizing between his toes, but he supposed that "better" was a relative term.

The breakfast hadn't been quite such a miracle cure for Brandon, but the food he was able to keep down really seemed to improve his color, and Dixie was pretty sure he even saw some blush in his cheeks before he ran back to work on the float. Or maybe it was a rash from exposure to the glue. Either way, Dixie appreciated the company.

Dixie walked inside and noticed the digital clock on Ms. Trasker's desk: he was two hours late to check in at the office. That's okay; Dixie wasn't going to the brig today, anyway. He still had a meth sample to steal and a drug cartel to expose, and he couldn't let a bunch of stapling and easy listening throw him off rhythm. Besides, with all the water damage and detectives at the office, he'd just get in the way.

He walked across the office to curl up under his desk for a strategy session/power nap but stopped before he could curl up against the industrial carpet. There was a long, clear plastic bag draped over his chair. Either somebody was planning on suffocating him with that, or his tuxedo had just arrived.

Dixie wasn't sure which one he'd prefer.

He lifted up the bag and looked through the plastic at the dark fabric inside. It was the tuxedo. So much for the sweet release of death.

A piece of paper dropped from the plastic bag and onto the carpet. Dixie picked it up:

> You better have a corsage, or there will be consequences. Dire. Consequences.
>
> Elaine
>
> P.S Shower. Shave. Comb. Deodorize. Or else!

Dixie tried to swallow, but couldn't force the saliva past the charcoal briquette lodged in his throat. So, the dance was tonight, was it? He was hoping that the tight ball of dread in his gut was just a tumor.

He slung the garment bag over his shoulder and walked out of the office to the bathroom in the basement of the Tower. The tuxedo wasn't really his style, but it was dry and clean, and like Nichols said, "next to the fountain pen, professional appearance is a reporter's most valuable tool."

Dixie stepped into the bathroom, changed in the handi-capped stall, and after fifteen minutes of vigorous scrubbing and a liberal amount of powdered soap, washed most of the grime off his face and hair. There were still bags under his eyes and flecks of soap-resistant dirt peppering his chin, but Dixie hoped that the classic lines of the tuxedo would dis-tract from all that. It seemed to work well enough for George Clooney.

"Whassup, tits?"

Dixie stared up at the strip of dirty windows near the ceiling that opened onto the quad. White twigs in Birkenstocks and sprouts of beefy khaki stood next to each other on the other side.

"Hey."

That was Funt and the albino.

Dixie smiled. This was the perfect opportunity for covert surveillance, and he didn't even have to risk bodily injury. It was about time his investigation started getting easier.

"You get some from Nicole last night?"

Dixie craned his neck and leaned forward but was too low to get an angle on his targets. He needed to get higher.

"Nah, I was carb loading," Funt said. "I wasn't really in the mood."

Dixie spotted the urinal beneath the window and sighed. It was a good thing these were rented shoes.

"Fag."

Dixie walked over, lifted his foot onto the urinal, and pulled himself up by the flush handle until he was safely perched on the porcelain rim.

"That's not faggy," Funt said. "I gotta play both ways now that Rick's foot's all jacked."

From Dixie's new perspective he could just make out the under cup of Funt's left breast.

"Damn." The albino chuckled. "That gook's freakin' dead."

Dixie tensed. He hoped they were talking about some gook besides himself, but wasn't too optimistic. He was pretty sure the guy who owned the fabric store was half Korean.

"Yeah."

Dixie shifted his weight forward to get a better vantage, and his right foot slipped forward into the urinal. As the liquid crested over his shoe and soaked into his sock, he decided that formal wear just wasn't designed for these kinds of maneuvers.

"Make sure you get plenty of this in you before the game."

Dixie looked up at the screen: the albino handed over a white envelope, and Funt tucked it into the side pocket of his cargo pants. This was worth the soggy socks and ruined patent leather—this was the drug handoff he'd been waiting for.

"Thanks," Funt said, patting against his pocket. "I'll need it."

The bathroom door creaked open, and Dixie turned. A red-faced butterball with a matching Hawaiian shirt stood in the entry, fumbling with his zipper, and staring at the dapper young man standing on the urinal.

Dixie nodded at the kid. "Howdy."

"Hey . . . why are you up there?"

Dixie looked at the butterball, then down to his submerged feet. "My shoes were dirty."

"Oh."

When he turned back to the screen, Funt and the albino were already walking through the quad and disappearing into the limited horizon. Dixie wasn't worried; he knew just where to find them. This was the day of a football game, and there was only one place in the world that Funt would be for the next forty-five minutes. After all, no self-respecting meathead would ever miss a pep rally.

Chapter 23

Friday, 11:28 a.m.

Dixie pushed open the side entrance to the gymnasium, waited for Coach Hamm to take his eyes off his security post to belch into his shirt collar, then squeezed between the narrow support beams under the bleachers and out of sight. Nobody noticed the intrusion; they were all too focused on the awkward dancing and loud music of the pep rally happening on the gym floor.

That was good—he was in the senior quarter of the gym, and it was normally suicide for an underclassman to cross class boundaries during a pep rally. Well, that was the rumor, at least. Unless he was on assignment, Dixie skipped the weekly jock worship for a quiet, extended lunch in the quad.

Today, he was on assignment.

Dixie bent over and waddled beneath the bleachers toward the severely taxed slat of wood that was supporting Funt's ass. He generally tried to avoid putting himself under any load-bearing structures built before the Kennedy administration, but he had to get close enough to Funt to steal the meth out of his pocket, and the possibility of getting crushed under the combined weight of the senior class and several tons of lumber still seemed like a much safer prospect than putting himself within mauling range of the football team.

"Yabba Dabba Doo! Here come the Wildcats to the rescue!"

Dixie shifted his head to a breach in the butt cheeks and looked out across the gym floor: Fred Flintstone and his dinosaur pals squared off with the rival high school's mascot at center court. Apparently, the Felton Mustang had stolen their football. Dixie was unsure what a horse wanted with such a thing, or how it all pertained to the Neolithic period of human development, but he didn't want to waste the distraction.

He snaked his arm under the bottom slot of the bleachers and up and around toward the bulge in Funt's pocket. This was it. Just two more inches to the right and three inches down, and he'd finally have enough evidence to prove his innocence and destroy the football team.

"Give us the ball, you Felton Mustang!"

That's when the lights turned off.

He should have expected that; no skit at Stilton High ended until the lights turned off and all manner of general chaos ensued in the name of school spirit.

Dixie pressed his shoulder against the bleachers to get a better angle on Funt's pocket. He reached inside and rooted around for the prize.

"Hey! Get off me!"

Dixie complied when he was sure that he wasn't holding any drugs, which was approximately the same instant he realized that he was fondling Funt's penis.

"What?" said a dark glob one space over.

"You grabbed my dick!"

"No I didn't. . . ." but his words slurred into a groan as Funt punched the suspected cock grabber in the face.

Dixie readjusted his aim and groped in the darkness one pocket forward. His fingers tucked into the fabric and brushed against something starchy. But before he could snag the package a foot swung down through the bleacher seats and knocked Dixie onto his ass.

He fell to the gym floor and watched the faint gray outline of the bleachers sway and creak above him as the punches spread and multiplied through the crowd.

This was bad.

Dixie turned around and crawled across the old candy and spilled soda beneath the bleachers to the distant red glow of the emergency exit sign. He pulled himself to his feet against the final support beam, lunged out the side doors, and sprinted around to the far side of the cafeteria before he remembered to start breathing.

Dixie leaned against the building, sucked back long pulls of wind, and took stock of what just happened:

Good: Was not trampled to death in riot.

Bad: Didn't get the drugs, touched Funt's penis, started riot, got tuxedo covered in dirt and old candy . . . pretty much everything besides not getting trampled to death.

Dixie reached up to brush a shard of Jolly Rancher off his forehead and noticed that his right hand was twisted into a fist. He hoped that wasn't something neurological. He just wasn't spiritually strong enough to survive in a world of southpaw masturbation.

He wedged his left index finger into the fist and pried open his hand. Something small and glass fell out of his grasp and tinkled onto the ground.

Dixie looked down at the object next to his sneakers. It was a medicine vial wrapped in a tattered strip of envelope.

"No way!"

He had caught something pocket fishing, after all. It was Funt's drugs.

Dixie picked it up and looked closer: a marijuana leaf was printed on the corner of the envelope and then again above Funt's name on the vial. The production values were surprisingly high for a meth cartel. Dixie hadn't expected Photoshop to be such an integral part of the business.

He tucked the shred of envelope securely between two pages of his notebook, and stared at the vial. Now he just had to figure out how to test this, and he could connect it back to the sick football players and Ralphino's cartel.

He twisted the vial against the sun to find its prism and sighed; this was probably going to be a lot more complicated than pocket fishing.

There were more meth-detection kits at the police station, but Dixie couldn't break in and steal one without a smoke bomb and a trained monkey, and his afternoon was already too backed up for such a complex operation. No, what he really needed was advice, some guidance from an expert in narcotic detection and chemical analysis—

Dixie looked across the street to the open door of Mr. Stone's classroom and squeezed the vial.

—Or, failing that, a Renaissance fair–enthusiast with some free time and a bachelor's degree in chemistry.

Chapter 24

Friday, 11:49 a.m.

Dixie stared through the open door of the classroom and found Mr. Stone sitting at his desk with his cheek draped over his shoulder and a fantasy-fiction book leaning against a display of beakers. Evidently, he wasn't much for pep rallies, either. That's good; establishing a common ground with the subject was an essential step in the interview process.

"Excuse me, Mr. Stone?" Dixie stepped inside and stopped in front of the desk. "Mr. Stone?"

Mr. Stone grunted from behind his paperback. On the front cover, a frog in a suit of armor stabbed at a dog wizard. Dixie made a mental note to check it out from the library as soon as his investigation quieted down. That looked like one hell of a story.

"Care to comment on homecoming, sir?"

Mr. Stone raised his eyes from his book and focused on Dixie. "Why are you wearing a tuxedo?"

He wasn't the first to ask that question, but "I'm a

Mormon," worked just fine with everyone else.

Mr. Stone nodded. "And who are you?"

Dixie. Dixie Nguyen. The highest grade in this class. The only person who memorized the periodic table. The one who set the lab on fire. That Dixie.

"I'm a reporter for the *Wildcat*," Dixie said. "Can I interview you about homecoming?"

Mr. Stone sighed and folded back the page of his paperback; the frog knight/dog wizard battle would have to wait. "Sure."

Dixie took out his notebook, opened to a blank page, and summoned up his most professional eyebrow furrow. He planned to start off with some easy questions. Gain some trust. Ease his prey into the kill zone.

"Do you like homecoming?" Dixie leaned in and tapped the base of his pen against his chin.

Mr. Stone breathed out long and low and ran his finger along the book's spine. Maybe he started out a bit *too* easy on that one. After all, he was competing against a world of anthropomorphic animals and thunderbolts.

"Sure . . . homecoming is an important, exciting time for every student."

Dixie nodded and decided to turn up the heat a bit with his next question. Just enough to keep things interesting.

"So, hypothetically speaking, suppose one of the students at homecoming, a cheerleader perhaps, was addicted to methamphetamines. . . . If a person got a hold of one of her needles, could he prove it was meth with the equipment in this lab, and if so, how?"

Mr. Stone stopped caressing the book. Tension built along the jawline. Sweat beaded on his eyebrows. A big, salty tear streaked down his cheek and rained down on the cover of his paperback.

"Get out," Mr. Stone said in a whisper. "Get the hell out, right now!"

"Excuse me?"

"I said to get the hell out."

This was all new territory to Dixie. Nichols didn't cover interviewing hostile subjects until the third edition, and the school couldn't afford the upgrade without selling the JV cheerleading squad to Saudi businessmen.

"How about off the record, then?" Dixie asked.

"Get her out of your filthy, goddamn mind."

"Her?" Dixie asked. "Look, she doesn't have to be a cheerleader, okay? Let's suppose the addict's some guy in the chess club."

Mr. Stone didn't say anything. He just kept turning more rigid and crimson. Dixie was fairly certain these were the symptoms of a heart attack, but he didn't want to jump the gun on calling for an ambulance. He had already made that mistake once in his life, and the paramedics were surprisingly uncool about it.

Mr. Stone hunched over and shook with sobs.

Dixie looked over his shoulder to the open door.

"I love her so much!" Mr. Stone said in a choked, muffled blubber from beneath the lumpy folds of skin on the desk.

Dixie stepped forward and stood next to Mr. Stone. He wanted to escape but was too much of a softie to abandon another man in the midst of an emotional grease fire.

"There, there . . . guy." Dixie reached out and gave a few comforting taps on Mr. Stone's shoulder. At least he assumed it was his shoulder; geographic specifics were difficult with a man of that size.

Mr. Stone lifted his head and stared at Dixie. His face was red and slick with tears and snot. Mostly snot. "What would you do?" he asked. "What would you do?"

"Do with what, sir?" Dixie asked, still patting Mr. Stone on the shoulder.

Mr. Stone grabbed Dixie's hand. "She hasn't been home in days. I . . . she's with them . . . that's where she always goes . . . and I . . ."

He doubled over into another crying fit, squeezing Dixie's hand.

"I'm sure she's okay." That wasn't strictly true, but Dixie figured that the better Mr. Stone felt, the less likely he was to break any fingers.

And thank Christ it worked.

"You . . . you really think that?" Mr. Stone loosed the tension on Dixie's hand ever so slightly.

"Sure!"

"You think my wife . . . she'll . . . my wife . . ." Then more crying. And squeezing. Mostly squeezing.

"Sure! She loves you! She loves you!"

Mr. Stone released Dixie's hand, then collapsed into another eruption of blubbering. Though it was difficult to decipher much through the sniffles and groans, Dixie was fairly certain that he heard "Sheryl," "TV," "pawn," and

"Eddie" in heavy rotation. Judging from the gnashing of teeth and surrounding growls, it appeared that he was particularly upset with this Eddie character.

Dixie filled in the blanks. His wife, Sheryl had pawn[ed] the TV for meth that she had purchased from Eddie whom she'd run off to have dirty, crank-fueled sex with.

"It's okay," Dixie said but kept his comfort pats verbal. "You're not alone."

Mr. Stone rolled his head to the side of the desk, peeked over his bicep, and howled something along the lines of "What?"

Dixie squinted his eyes and scrunched his forehead, or in the words of the drama teacher at the community center, emoted. "My mom sold my bicycle for meth last week. . . . I know what you're going through."

"Really?"

"That's why I came to you," Dixie said, and diverted all reserve mental energy toward a lip quiver. "I didn't know where else to turn. . . . Help me find help . . . for her."

Mr. Stone nodded, stood up from his chair, and lumbered around the desk.

"Here, take this," Mr. Stone said. "It might help you."

Mr. Stone extended a brochure to Dixie. "This is a company that helps people in our . . . situation."

Dixie looked down at the brochure: there was a watercolor of a sun rising over a meadow on the front page, with HAMILTECH DIAGNOSTICS in big red letters curving across the top.

"Send them some of your mom's drugs, and they'll let

you know what you're dealing with," Mr. Stone said.

Dixie nodded, flipped the brochure around to the EXPEDITED TESTING RATES and felt his testicles plummet to his kneecaps. He didn't have enough money for a postage stamp, let alone the $378 it was going to cost to get Funt's drugs tested in time for the hearing on Monday.

He looked out the open door and saw the top floor of the Tower crest over the droopy trees and auditorium across the street and smiled; it was a good thing this was a business expense. Ms. Trasker kept her school-issued "supplies" credit card in the top drawer of the *Wildcat* office, and though the funds were already earmarked for the newspaper staff party, Dixie felt his freedom was a slightly more pressing concern than some Red Baron Pizza and grape soda.

"Thank you." Dixie folded the brochure into his pocket and edged toward the door. "And best of luck with all that other stuff."

Mr. Stone didn't move.

"So, I guess I'll be going now," Dixie circled around Mr. Stone's girth toward the open door but quickly regretted stepping inside the man's grasping range.

"We're gonna be okay." Mr. Stone squeezed Dixie's head between his breasts. "We're gonna be okay."

Dixie relaxed his neck muscles and nuzzled against Mr. Stone's chest. He might as well take the opportunity to rest; he had one hell of a busy afternoon coming up. There were stories to write and credit cards to steal and drug tests to order and a long, fast march down to the post office before it shut down for the day.

He closed his eyes, breathed deep into Mr. Stone's musk, and hoped that these hugs wouldn't become too regular in his interactions with the man. The other students would never understand the complexities of their relationship.

Chapter 25

Friday, 1:20 p.m.

Dixie sprawled across the wooden bench in front of the post office and looked over at the neon sign of the discount grocery store across the street. A quick trip inside for a bottle of Gatorade and some Dr. Scholl's comfort insoles might have been best for Dixie's mental state and podiatric well-being (tuxedo shoes just weren't designed for the realities of prolonged athletic movement), but after the most recent charges to Ms. Trasker's credit card (express diagnostic from Hamiltech—$378. Priority shipping to Miami, FL—$29) he felt it was best to stay frugal with his purchases for the foreseeable future. At least until he won the Pulitzer, pawned the trophy for folding money, and paid off Ms. Trasker's Visa bill before she noticed the charges.

He balled his tuxedo jacket into a pillow and snuggled against the fabric. His feet hurt and he was chancing homicide from a menopausal editor, but all that didn't matter now. His investigation was finished.

Sure he still didn't have all the answers—he didn't know *why* Ralphino was supplying the team with meth, or *how* the football players ended up in the hospital—but when the results came back from Hamiltech, he could finally prove that everything was connected.

And although his work didn't quite pass Nichols's test, Dixie had the foundation for a perfectly serviceable story, and hopefully enough evidence to prove his innocence at the hearing on Monday. If the OJ Simpson trial had taught Dixie anything, it was that the average American had a generous definition of "reasonable doubt." Also, the average American is an idiot.

Dixie rolled onto his side and hugged his knees to his chest. All that was left was waiting for the results from Hamiltech, grinding out a rough draft of his article, and watching a few back episodes of *Boston Legal* to prep for his hearing. But for now, Dixie felt it was best to start things off with a nap.

Just a power nap, fifteen minutes to recharge the batteries, and then he'd get right back to work. Well, maybe he could squeeze in a quick detour back to the high school to share the good news with Brynn. Dixie folded the arms of the tuxedo jacket over his eyes to block out the sun and smiled. Maybe he'd even get another kiss.

"Wake up."

Dixie unfolded the tuxedo arms out of his face and opened his eyes: it was dark and a policeman stood over him. Well, this was different. He must have lost control of the power nap. That was the real risk of the maneuver.

"Hello, sir," Dixie said.

That wasn't just any policeman; it was his father.

"Are you okay?" the sergeant asked.

Dixie didn't expect that question or really anything besides a nightstick to his shin. The sergeant would never allow a family crime so severe as ditching class or loitering in front of a government building to pass without some form of physical damage.

"I'm just a little tired, that's all."

"Move your legs, Dixie."

Dixie cooperated. He didn't have the energy to fight or run or beg for his shins.

But the sergeant kept the nightstick in his utility belt. Instead, he sat down on the bench and cleared his throat.

"I'm sorry," the sergeant said.

Dixie wasn't familiar with this type of torture, but guessed that it was psychological. "Excuse me?"

"I know what happened at the spaghetti feed was an accident, and I shouldn't have left you. That was wrong."

Well, this was a flip from the family's standard apology dynamic. "That's okay."

"No, it's not, Dixie," the sergeant said. "I was an asshole last night. . . . I've been an asshole all week."

"Uhh . . . okay?" Outside of lawn care and stubbed toes, it was the first time that Dixie had ever heard his father curse. He hoped that it wouldn't become too regular an occurrence in their interactions; he enjoyed the formality of Sunday dinners.

"I didn't know you were having so many problems." The sergeant's radio squawked, but he turned a dial until it went silent. "It's tough with a kid like you. . . . I guess I just figured you were smart enough to take care of yourself."

The sergeant reached over and patted Dixie on the knee. It was a sweet gesture, and Dixie really wished that he hadn't flinched.

"I want you to talk to me . . . you know, the next time you're having problems." The sergeant reached up and squeezed Dixie's shoulder. "I want to help."

Dixie nodded. "Okay." He appreciated his father's offer and intended to make use of it in the future, but felt it was best not to bring the sergeant into his current situation. He didn't want to ruin the sentimentality of the moment with a bunch of "meth cartel" and "jock vendetta" talk.

He compromised by leaning in and giving his father a hug.

"I love you, son," the sergeant said. "Even if you are a junkie."

Dixie squeezed back a little harder. "Me too."

After a few seconds, and a final, lung-clearing squeeze, the sergeant pulled back and looked at Dixie. "Aren't you supposed to be at the game?"

Dixie looked down at his digital watch: the game had kicked off thirty minutes earlier.

"Shit!" Dixie said, and from the sergeant's eyebrow tilt, decided that he still wasn't quite ready to join his father in the world of manly swearing. Perhaps when he leased his first truck. "Sorry."

"Come on." The sergeant stood up off the bench

and offered Dixie his hand. "We'll take the cruiser."

"Really?"

The sergeant pulled Dixie to his feet. "Somebody's got to write about the game, right?"

Dixie smiled. Yes, somebody did. Somebody was still the chief sports correspondent for the *Stilton High Wildcat* and damned proud to do his job.

"Can I borrow ten dollars?" Dixie asked.

And that somebody had to pop into the grocery store for a disposable camera.

Chapter 26

The game was already a rout for the visiting team when Dixie flashed his press pass and stepped through the entrance gate to the football field. And though he could understand the ticket lady's frustration over losing a potential sale, the "You go to hell," she spat at him as he passed seemed a bit excessive. She must be working on commission.

But as Dixie cut through the grass to the concessions shack for his "journalism power" cup of hot cocoa, it seemed that everyone queued for the Porta Potties followed his progress with hateful glares. Or maybe they were discomfort glares. The football field was designed with only enough bathroom facilities to accommodate a family of four, and the painful realities of large crowds, chili nachos, and portable toilets was enough to knock the rainbow out of anyone's day.

He ordered his cocoa and noticed the day's *Stilton Gazette* leaning against a cauldron of nacho cheese sauce inside the snack shack. He was too far away to read the fine print, but the bold type on the front page was clear enough: SPASTIC YOUTH BREAKS STAR LINEBACKER'S FOOT with an enlarged reproduction of Dixie's yearbook photo positioned beneath the headline.

Well, that would explain the crowd's hatred, and Dixie decided that a summer internship at the local newspaper wasn't too likely, either. Maybe Taco Bell was hiring.

"Take your damn cocoa!"

Dixie looked up from the headline: a wildebeest wearing too much rouge and an apron pushed a Styrofoam cup of cocoa across the counter and scowled at Dixie until he handed over a dollar.

He grabbed the drink and stepped out of line. He would have preferred to grab a few extra napkins and a packet of NutraSweet off the condiment station, but he felt it was a better idea to step outside the range of the snack-shack lady's brisket fork.

Dixie walked to the roped off boundary of the football field and snapped a picture of two of the larger specimens nosing into each other by the goal line. He was safer here. The yelling of the crowd was indistinguishable over the pop of colliding helmets, and the angry eyes in the audience faded to white against the bright shine of the light posts.

A gun sounded to end the quarter. Dixie flinched at the noise, spilling cocoa onto his tuxedo shirt. He watched the cocoa stain join the developing mosaic of old candy and dirt, and made a mental note to order his next tuxedo with a matching bib.

The public address system crackled and filled the

stadium. "And now, ladies and gentlemen, please join me in honoring the boosters whose generosity made this new field a reality: Larry Mosson, Gerald England, Jim Nielsen, and Daniel Ralphino."

Upon hearing "Ralphino," Dixie dropped the rest of his cocoa onto his shoes. It was a shame to waste the beverage, especially one that was so close to complete marshmallow osmosis, but Dixie needed both of his hands at the moment.

He pulled out his notebook and flipped to the Six W page; maybe his story wasn't quite so "finished," after all.

WHY: Ralphino sold meth to pay for the new football field.

Ralphino wasn't just a meth kingpin. He was the most involved booster in the history of high-school athletics. Everything about the cartel was designed to help the team: the inferior drugs were sold to hobos to pay for the new field, the team got supplied with the good meth, and the cycle would keep running for each new season.

Dixie looked out onto the field: a group of old men in Stilton High jackets walked out onto the fifty-yard line.

He pulled the camera out of his jacket and cranked back the loading wheel. This was the perfect conspiracy, the kind of story that came along once in a career, and he was just one headline photograph from completing the scoop.

Dixie ducked under the rope, sprinted onto the field, and lowered to one knee to get the scoreboard in frame with the old men.

"Gerald England, Jim Nielsen, Larry Mosson . . ."

Down the line, each man stepped forward to receive the crowd's applause, and Dixie's trigger finger twitched with each passing name.

"Daniel Ralphino . . ."

Dixie spasmed with excitement, farted, clicked down on the camera—

". . . could not be here tonight due to a prior engagement."

—And took a picture of plastic grass and empty space.

He stared at the blank spot where the meth kingpin was supposed to be until the applause ended and the men shuffled off the field. Prior commitment? What else could Ralphino have planned that was more important than this? He couldn't have taken over local meth production and funneled the profits to finance a new football field just because he was getting tired of shuffleboard. No, none of this made any sense. Not unless . . .

"Oh shit."

Ralphino didn't exist.

He was just a name. A cover. Legal protection for whoever was really running the meth cartel, and Dixie wasn't a good enough reporter to see it.

Dixie dropped his camera onto the turf and shuffled off to the sideline. This was bad. Without a kingpin to tie it all together, he didn't have a scoop—just some crank-addicted jocks, a few coincidences, and a skinny dork that got in over his head.

He was screwed.

Dixie stepped off the field onto the track and felt a low rumble building in his direction. He turned to the noise and closed his eyes. So, here came the jock retribution. He was surprised it had taken them so long.

"Out of my way, pervert!"

Something large and fleshy crashed into Dixie's chest and sent him skidding across the dirt track. He rolled over and waited for the plastic spikes to circle around and end the pain, but instead, his assailant ran down the track and disappeared into the darkness beyond the football field.

The mercy was unexpected, as was the skirt and the generous application of mascara.

That was Julie.

"Hey, Dixie."

He looked over: Brandon sat on the grass a few feet past the track and leaned back against the senior float.

Dixie pushed himself to his feet and walked over to the float. Considering the state of his investigation, he probably should have spent his time packing or buying a bus ticket to Tijuana, but Dixie wanted to get in some quality time with his brother before starting life as a fugitive. He had a feeling that he wouldn't be seeing much of his family for a while.

"Uh . . . so, what's going on with Julie?" Dixie asked.

"Homecoming didn't go quite as well as she wanted." Brandon motioned to a large, gold trophy perched next to Scooby Doo's magical mystery van on the sophomore float. "She was pretty upset."

"Oh. So, are you guys still . . ." Dixie started, but trailed off before he could finish. He wasn't sure if what they were doing was exactly dating, but "doing it" just didn't seem quite sensitive enough, either.

Brandon shook his head. "Nah, I don't think so. . . ." Water accumulated in his eyes, but he shrugged it off before they dripped down into tears. "How's the investigation going?"

"Well . . . ," Dixie tried to speak but couldn't force the words past the lump building in his throat. He compromised by taking the notebook out of his back pocket and throwing it onto the ground.

"Oh," Brandon said.

Dixie slumped over onto the float and buried his face into the Astro Turf between a potted azalea and papier-mâché volcano. The notebook toss was a bit dramatic for his tastes, but he didn't really need it. Not anymore. What he needed was a sturdy pair of hiking boots or a lobotomy, anything to make his time at VisionQuest go a little smoother.

"What's this?" Brandon asked.

Dixie lifted his face from the float and looked down: Brandon lifted the corner of Funt's envelope out of the notebook and held it against the illumination of the field lights.

"Nothing." Dixie dropped his face back into the Astro Turf. "Just some stationery for the meth cartel. Pretty cool pot leaf, huh?"

"That's not a pot leaf."

Dixie rolled to his cheek and looked down at his brother. "What?"

Brandon held up the scrap of envelope. "This is the Canadian flag."

Dixie snatched the paper out of Brandon's hand and held it up to the light. So it was. He made a mental note to schedule an appointment with the optometrist; his prescription needed a significant upgrade.

"Would you mind handing me that notebook?" Dixie asked.

This was big, even the possibility of macular degeneration couldn't dampen the moment. His investigation was still alive.

Brandon handed over the notebook and Dixie flipped it open to the Six W page:

HOW: Meth kingpin (Ralphino?) imported
meth from Canadian syndicate
disguised as prescription drugs.

Dixie looked at the last entry and smiled. This was the biggest scandal in the history of US-Canada relations since Alex Trebek took all that acid and bit the head off a chicken at the Astrodome. Or maybe that was Ozzy Osbourne. Dixie always had a dickens of a time keeping those two straight.

But he still couldn't prove it. Not yet.

He couldn't chance an international incident with America's number one supplier of lumber and daytime television actors using just a scrap of envelope and some wild stories. No, he needed concrete evidence. Some indisputable proof of the Canadian cartel's existence and their connection to the football team: an address, an invoice, anything—

Dixie tucked the notebook into his pocket and looked across the field to the dark outline of the locker room.

—And he knew just where to find it.

"You okay?" Brandon asked.

"Very okay." Dixie clapped his brother on the shoulder and stepped back onto the track. "See you at the dance."

Dixie jogged across the track, stepped through the damp grass of the softball field, and stopped in front of the locker room.

It was crazy to go in there. The football team would be heading inside for their post-game showers and meth binge soon, and if he wasn't careful, he'd get trapped with several dozen naked crank addicts who wanted to kill him. The only sensible move was to go someplace safe and wait for his hearing on Monday.

He breathed deep and grabbed the door handle.

But he had gone through too much this week to walk away now.

Dixie pulled open the door and stepped into the locker room.

It was time to finish this thing.

Chapter 27

Friday, 7:05 p.m.

The door to the locker room was unlocked, and after a short detour to the bathroom to wash the cocoa off his hands, Dixie walked into the varsity room and started his investigation. That's when the trouble started.

There wasn't anything incriminating in the balled-up athletic tape and paper cups on the floor, or the squiggles on the chalkboard, and he was having some difficulty with breaking into the lockers. More precisely, he had never picked a lock before in his life and had no idea what he was doing.

After twenty minutes of kicking, psychic projection, and twirling the dials until his fingertips chafed, Dixie had only been able to open Rick's locker, and that was only because they shared a combination. Unfortunately, Rick's locker was clean. At least devoid of incriminating evidence. There was still enough dirt and pornography stashed inside to supply a dozen adolescents and their tree forts, but that was normal enough.

Dixie sat down, and leaned his head against the locker's metal grate; it was probably time to start thinking through some alternate strategies:

Plan A: Steal car. Drive across Canadian border. Locate meth distributor.

Sure, Canada was a big country, but most of it was snow and doughnut shops, anyway, so Dixie figured his odds of bumping into the meth distributor had to be just as good as breaking into one of these lockers. Plus, if his investigation hit any snags, he could always work as a fur trapper in the Yukon wilderness until the trouble blew over. Maybe. He'd have to check on their extradition laws.

Dixie leaned over and punched the hinge on the neighboring locker. That was Plan B. Unfortunately, besides the skin across his knuckles, that didn't open anything, either.

A door slammed somewhere in the locker room, and Dixie's sphincter wasn't far behind. One of the football players was in the locker room.

This was bad.

Dixie jumped to his feet and scanned the room for exits. The front door would put him in the direct path of whoever just came inside, and there weren't any windows or air-conditioning vents for high altitude escapes. That was probably for the best; Dixie had trouble with heights. More specifically, falling from them.

He turned and studied the dimensions of the open locker. He was hoping it wouldn't come to this, but that was his best chance for concealment, and he knew that he'd fit inside with enough pushing. His fellows in the locker room were kind enough to have cleared up any doubt about that possibility on the first day of school. Also the fifth and thirty-eighth. Whenever the fancy struck them, really.

The footsteps were ten feet from the door. Seven. Four.

"Oh, what the hell." Dixie turned and wedged himself ass-first into the locker. He folded his shoulders back against the sides of the container and had just enough remaining mobility to stick his pinky through the ventilation meshing and settle the door back against the locking mechanism, but stopped before it latched. Hiding was one thing, trapping himself in a three foot square box, a different matter entirely.

The footsteps stopped in front of the door. The sleeve of a blue industrial jumpsuit snaked through the open door, and the hand inside flicked the light switch. The door closed. The footsteps clinked away.

Dixie released his breath in short, loud gasps. The threat hadn't been quite so severe as he anticipated, but he was glad to see that the school's janitors were focused on conserving natural resources.

Now, back to the investigation.

Dixie shifted his weight to free his hand, and his knee bumped against the side of the locker.

That's when he heard the click.

"Uh-oh." He had just trapped himself inside the locker. It would almost be comical, if it weren't for the possibility of asphyxiation.

Dixie closed his eyes and slowed his breathing. This wasn't his finest moment as an investigative reporter, but he couldn't let the negative energy cloud his thinking. It took focus from the here and now, and both were complicated enough to deserve his full and undivided attention:

1. He was stuck inside a locker.

2. His nose itched.

3. His finger couldn't reach that high.

Yep, this was going to take a thorough pondering, but he had plenty of time for that. At least three days. Dixie was pretty sure he could survive that long without any water.

Chapter 28

Friday, 8:58 p.m.

Dixie strained his arm and forehead against the metal sides of the locker to get a look at his wristwatch but couldn't get the right angle without popping his shoulder out of alignment. That was okay; he didn't need to know the exact hour, anyway. He was already late to the dance. His bladder wouldn't be pressing so urgently against his waistband if he hadn't been stuck in there for at least a couple of hours.

Ms. Trasker would be annoyed. That, or she would rip off his scrotum with her back teeth. Dixie supposed it all depended on how much gin she had in the system.

Of course, until somebody wandered into the locker room and took pity on his situation, the exact manifestation of Trasker's revenge was purely academic. But no one had entered. Well, besides the expected twenty minutes of penises and yelling when the football players came in to change after the game, but everybody was a little too naked and angry for his tastes, and at that moment, Dixie felt a bit more comfortable staying inside the locker.

He felt differently now. Dixie was willing to risk the gang beating from the football team (at least he hoped that "beating" was the most sinister verb he'd have to contend with) or the improvised vasectomy from Ms. Trasker, anything to get out of this locker.

Dixie heard muffled voices and footsteps outside the door of the locker room, and smiled. Somebody was finally here to rescue him. That, or beat him to death. Of course, so long as he got to stretch his legs, either option sounded nice enough.

The door twisted open: five tuxedo shoes and two crutches clinked inside.

"I don't know, his mom's uncle, or his uncle's dad or something. Who cares? It's a party on a lake house, man!" The crutcher's voice cracked an octave with the exclamation. "What the hell do you want?"

Dixie pulled back into the darkness. That was Rick. Suddenly, staying inside the locker for the rest of his life didn't seem so bad, after all.

"Who cares if it's on a lake?" It was the albino's voice. "It's night, you idiot."

"Whatever, it's just romantic is all," Rick said. "And dude, there's gonna be so much drunk and willing tang over there, even a chunky bastard like Funt could get laid."

Besides, Dixie would hate to interrupt such an involved and sophisticated conversation. It was just bad manners.

"Nah, he wouldn't be interested in that," the albino said. "He's got a steady."

"I don't got a steady!" Funt said.

"Yeah, well Nicole sure bought you a nice corsage for being her fuddy."

Dixie heard the click of a lighter and the soft crackle of burning leaves.

"Funt, you're dating Nicole?" Rick asked. "Really?"

Dixie had never smelled tobacco like that before but guessed that it came from a pipe. Not that he had a wide frame of reference on the subject. The only person who ever smoked a pipe in front of him was his grandpa, and his tobacco smelled like tobacco. The funny smell was entirely his own.

"Talking," Funt said. "We're just talking."

"Dude, she totally gave me a handjob in junior high!" Rick said. "That's awesome! We're like half milk brothers!"

"Shut up!"

"Do you think I can still get in on that?" Rick asked. "I don't mind if you watch. That'd be kinda hot, actually."

So, this was how friends talked about their romances. Dixie supposed that was one of the benefits of not having any friends.

Rick's crutches circled around Funt's shoes, and the albino laughed.

"Get off me!"

"How am I supposed to control myself around these big titties?"

"Knock it off!"

"I love titties!"

There was a grunt and then something shattered on the ground.

"What the hell?"

"Sorry, dude."

"That pipe cost me, like, thirty bucks," the albino said.

"I said I was sorry. If Funt didn't have such a bitch grip, we wouldn't even have this problem."

"I'm not even buzzed yet," Funt said.

"Chill." The crutches turned and clinked toward Dixie's locker. "I've got a bottle of schnapps in my locker."

So, it's a bottle. Dixie was wondering what had been jabbing up his ass for the last couple hours.

"I'm not drinking that girly stuff," the albino said.

"Why not?" Rick crouched down and eclipsed the locker's ventilation slits. "It tastes like an apple."

The hinges squeaked and locker door swung open.

"What the hell?"

There wasn't much good to be taken from his current situation, but Dixie appreciated the influx of fresh air into the locker. He had almost forgotten there was a whole world out there that mostly didn't smell like Rick's undergarments.

"Hey! What are you doing in my locker, pixie dick?"

But that wasn't the world Dixie was in. At least not yet.

"I said, what the hell are you doing in my locker?" Rick stabbed his crutch into Dixie's thigh. At least he assumed it was his thigh. Loss of sensation in the extremities was an unexpected benefit from his confinement.

"Relax, you moron," Dixie said. "I'm thinking."

Rick sucked his upper lip into his gums and inhaled through his teeth.

Dixie took a deep breath and swallowed the remaining moisture in his mouth. He recognized that look and knew what was coming next: he was about to take a beating. All that left was making sure this would be a standard, rage-motivated beating and not one of the sadistic, cry for help, sexual, physical, mental, and anything else that could be done to the human body with a broomstick variety.

"Rick, your mother is a woman of low character, and I have it on authority that your grandfather molests stray cats."

From the blush in Rick's cheeks and the flare of his nostrils, it appeared that the rage plan was a success.

Dixie closed his eyes and took a moment to appreciate the few, blissful moments before the pain started. He was pretty sure there wouldn't be too many more of these before the night was through.

Chapter 29

Friday, 9:12 p.m.

A stream of cold water douched Dixie's naked body, and snapped him back into consciousness. Or maybe it was his face slamming into the shower tiles that did the snapping.

Rick reached up and twisted off the stream of water. "You like that, pixie dick?"

Dixie rolled out of the water and looked up at Rick. He was cold, his body hurt, and Lord knows what manner of bacteria was jumping up from the tiles and colonizing in his pores. No, as a matter of fact, there was very little he liked about his current situation.

"Where are my clothes?"

Rick smiled and Dixie cringed. He knew that look.

"I pooped on them," Rick said.

Dixie nodded. Well, that cleared up any lingering doubt.

"You might want to think about changing up your routine," Dixie said, pushing up to his feet. "You're starting to get a bit predictable."

Rick pointed his crutch at Dixie's chest and spit. "I'll do whatever I want, you goddamn queer!"

Dixie heard the faint sounds of "slut" and "no" and "deviant" and "no" over the hiss of the water, and tilted his view around Rick's body into the bathroom. Funt's pants were bunched around his ankles, and the albino stabbed a hypodermic needle into his left buttock. Dixie appreciated their consistency; it was a real comfort in these troubled times.

"Look at me, queer bait."

Dixie felt a sharp pain in his foot and looked down: Rick pressed the plastic tip of his crutch onto Dixie's big toe and twisted.

Dixie jumped back, but Rick crutched forward onto the shower tiles.

"Me and you still gotta straighten out a few things," Rick said.

"Like?"

"Like you broke my foot, cocksucker!" Rick screamed, pounding his crutch down next to his cast.

"Oh, that . . ." Dixie inched backward. "Sorry about that."

He wasn't. In fact, breaking Rick's foot was one of the few moments of pure joy that he had ever experienced, but Dixie felt it was best not to complicate the situation with the truth, just then.

Rick showed his fangs and crutched forward. "Not good enough."

Dixie stepped back until his shoulders pressed against the shower wall. It felt strange to be terrified of the physically disabled, but these were desperate and confusing times. So desperate and confusing, in fact, that Dixie almost didn't feel embarrassed about what he was about to do next.

"Stay back!" Dixie fished his penis from the protective folds of his scrotum, and he pointed the nozzle at Rick. "I'll do it!"

"What? Jack off? I'd like to see that." Rick smiled—but this one wasn't so familiar to Dixie. It was tense, hungry, dangerous. Dixie imagined it was the last thing a whole crop of sad girls saw in the dying moments of their virginity. That, and the roof of his truck.

"I'll piss on you." It was a bluff. Dixie could never urinate with another guy watching, let alone with such damp and chilled equipment, but Rick didn't know that, and that was the real beauty of the maneuver.

Rick's smile drooped, and he stopped crutching forward. "No you won't."

"Try me."

"I'll kill you if you piss on me." That wasn't a bluff.

Rick shifted his weight to his good leg and tightened his grip on the crutches. He was ready to attack. So was Dixie.

"Go ahead." Dixie stepped forward. "We'll see who's quicker."

"Whatever." Rick shuffled off the shower tiles and then looked up from his crutches. His lips twisted into a smirk, and a dark twinkle sparked in his eye. "Hey, you still going with that chubby slut?"

Dixie felt his testicles suck back into his stomach, but it wasn't just the cold water. Rick was talking about Brynn.

"She's been following me around for months." Rick chuckled and clicked his tongue off the roof of his mouth. "Maybe it's time I gave her some more of what she's been begging for."

Dixie's chest tingled and his eyeballs burned with rage, but he didn't know if he was angry because of what Rick was saying—

"Ain't no pussy like them stoner bitches. They're just happy for the attention."

—Or because he thought it was true.

Brynn wasn't at the spaghetti feed for the noodles. She wasn't at the night rally to steal wallets. She didn't go to the convenience store for the soda.

She was following Rick.

"It's been a while since she had a taste." Rick grabbed his crotch and ran his tongue along the track of his mustache. "I don't want her to forget what a real man feels like."

Rick opened his mouth to laugh, but Dixie couldn't hear it. Not with the seismic thumps in his chest and the slow grind in his jaw.

"Leave her alone!" Dixie lunged for Rick's face, but his feet slipped against the slick tiles, and he flopped forward onto his stomach before he could scratch out any eyeballs.

"What a fucking geek!" Rick laughed and crutched down the aisle of lockers toward the exit. "Let's go, guys!"

A toilet flushed. More footsteps followed behind. The door creaked open and closed.

They were gone.

Dixie rolled back onto the cold, slimy tiles and stared up

at the ceiling. He had failed. He wasn't a good enough reporter to tie the investigation together, and he was out of time. Nothing he did was going to make any difference. The cartel would keep selling, the football team would keep winning, and the homeless would keep dying.

He was just a pest. A minor annoyance. An amateur who didn't do anything but hurt the people he loved.

Like Brynn.

Dixie closed his eyes and bit down until his cheeks shook. Rick was going to use her, and discard her and he couldn't stop it.

Unless . . .

Dixie opened his eyes and released the death grip in his jaw. There might still be one way to fix this.

He pushed to his feet and walked to the bathroom. The investigation was ruined, and he was going to VisionQuest, but Dixie wasn't ready to give up quite yet. Not when Rick still had two functional testicles, and there were so many perfectly good blunt weapons in the world.

Dixie stopped at the faucets and scanned the room for any loose brick or exposed pipe. The testicle smash might not be the right move journalistically, but some things were more important than his professional reputation, and saving the world from Rick's sperm had to be one of them.

He looked past the faucets and noticed a series of black scribbles on the mirror: BRYNN IS A SLUT.

He stared at the mirror, and his hand spasmed into a fist. There was no sense in leaving that around, either.

Dixie aimed for SLUT, crashed his knuckles into the

mirror, and immediately gained a newfound respect for the durability of industrial glass.

He bent over to clutch his fist and noticed a familiar red glint at the bottom of the trash can. "No way!"

Dixie reached his non-mangled hand past the damp paper towels, athletic tape, and hypodermic needle in its container, grabbed the package, and set it down on the sink. A return address was printed beneath the Canadian flag:

Great White North Pharmaceuticals
18 West Elsinore Drive
Hamilton, Ontario
Canada

Dixie reached back and patted the cold, damp flesh of his left buttock, then remembered that his notebook was currently marinating in the center toilet stall, along with the rest of his tuxedo and whatever Rick ate for breakfast.

That was okay, though; Dixie didn't need to write this down, anyway. His investigation was finished.

He picked up the package and twisted it around to see every angle. This was it: final proof of the cartel's existence and enough evidence to write a Pulitzer-caliber article, prove his innocence, and destroy the football team and their meth cartel.

This was the perfect story, the kind of scoop that came along once in a career—

Dixie tucked the package under his arm and walked out of the bathroom.

—But that just wasn't good enough. Not anymore.

The investigation and trial would take months, maybe even years, and Dixie couldn't let Rick and the rest of those assholes go unpunished for that long.

He needed to let everyone in Stilton know just what kind of scum they were worshipping. He needed to make sure that no girl like Brynn would ever get seduced by one of those meatheads, ever again. He needed to hurt the football team at least as bad as a steel pipe to the balls.

And nothing spread that kind of news faster than word of mouth.

Dixie walked down the rows of lockers and stopped at the door to the gymnasium. Low bass and the scuffling of rented shoes leaked through from the other side. The homecoming dance was in full swing, and that's where the county's mouths were gathered tonight.

Dixie looked down at his cold, wet flesh and sighed; this was a bad time to be naked and shriveled.

He ripped a spirit poster off the wall, looped the butcher paper from shoulder to crotch, and tucked it secure against his wrist. He hated to destroy an artist's creation, even one who worked in sparkly paint, but he had an important announcement to make and needed the coverage.

Besides, if people didn't know that *Wildcats Rule!* by now, they probably never would.

Chapter 30

Friday, 9:32 p.m.

Dixie stepped into the gymnasium, crouched behind a decorative balloon arrangement, and surveyed the room. The dancers bunched around a small stage in the center of the gym floor, and a spotlight shone down on a portly man stuffed into business casual. Dixie recognized him as Mark, the male half of the town's most popular AM radio morning-chat show. Rumor was that the female half was unable to attend due to a prior engagement with a bottle of Asti Spumante, the VHS of her wedding, and a cat named Mittens.

Mark mopped off his jowl sweat, unfastened the microphone from the stand, and stepped forward into the disk of light. "All right, Stilton High, and now the moment you've all been waiting for!"

The audience cheered and inched closer to the stage.

Mark pulled out two envelopes from the breast pocket of his blazer. "The winner of this year's homecoming queen competition, as voted by her peers is . . ."

Mark paused to rip open the envelope to retrieve the name inside. It was a waste of perfectly good office supplies—everyone knew who was going to win. The men in attendance (teachers included) had already edged themselves next to the stage to maximize their view of the jiggle.

"Sarah Irving!"

They weren't disappointed.

Sarah didn't appear too surprised by the selection, either, but still emoted enough to make the moment feel right, and while her hops of joy across the stage may have been a bit gratuitous, the lucky fellows in the splash zone below appreciated the gesture.

Dixie was enjoying the show himself until two people careened into the balloon arrangement next to him and settled against the wall.

The couple circled around to get a better attack angle on each other's tonsils, and the strobe light swept across the face of her partner.

"Holy crap."

That was Ms. Trasker.

"Double holy crap."

And she was kissing Huggy Bear. Dixie was sure of it. He was the only person in the county who owned a hemp tuxedo.

Evidently, this was why lonely women weren't supposed to be alone at social functions. But at least they made sense as a couple, and it was somehow appropriate that Ms. Trasker ended up with a substance abuse counselor. Dixie assumed that Huggy Bear probably had some kind of discount arrangement for friends and family.

They rolled against the wall decorations, leaned against the side door, and stumbled into the darkness toward Huggy Bear's healing space. Dixie was glad that his two mentors had found each other but still made a mental note to avoid any physical contact with the beanbags for the foreseeable future, at least not until they had gone through a professional dry cleaning and exorcism.

"And now, this year's homecoming king, as chosen by his peers to represent Stilton High, is . . ."

Dixie turned back to the stage. The audience shuffled back and cleared a path for Rick to crutch up to the stage. There weren't any surprises here, either. They knew he was king. He would always be king. The world was just too damned cruel for him not to hold some kind of leadership position.

Just not tonight. Tonight was about justice.

"The winner is . . . Brandon Presto."

Tonight was for the little guy.

Rick pumped his crutches in the air, and the audience accompanied him with applause until the incongruence set in:

Rick Johnson wasn't the king.

Brandon Presto was the king.

And just who the hell was Brandon Presto, anyway?

Rick lowered his crutches and hobbled into the shadows beyond the stage. Dixie hoped that he wouldn't go too far; the night's humiliation was just getting started.

"Brandon Presto?" Mark cupped his hand over the glare of the spotlight and looked into the audience. "Is Brandon here?"

Dixie scanned through the gymnasium for his brother; just where in the hell was the "little guy" anyway? The whole point of the election fraud was to get his brother some public adulation. Dixie hoped they would still let Brandon keep the crown; that was sure to make for a nifty conversation starter.

"Has anyone found Brandon? We have a crown for him."

Dixie stepped out from behind the balloons and stared up at the stage. Brandon must be too busy to collect his crown, but that was okay. There'd be a Presto family representative up there soon enough.

"What are you wearing?"

Dixie looked over to the voice: a short Hawaiian girl in a plaid skirt stared back, along with her date and everyone else in a ten-foot radius.

"Wildcats rule!" Dixie said, and charged into the crowd.

Dixie forced his way through the gaps between the first few layers of people, but the core in front of the stage was far too dense to penetrate by conventional means.

He ducked under the arm bridge of a hand-holding couple and cleared his throat; this was going to take some voice projection. "Cock waffles! I've got the bug inside me!"

Maybe in the more sophisticated and urban areas of the world, people wouldn't give much space to a battered, incoherent man dressed in paper, but this was the mountains, and thank God for small towns.

Dixie reached the stage, and coiled his leg muscles, but something grabbed his arm and pulled him back before he could leap.

"Stop it!"

Dixie turned back: Principal Restano was that something.

He looked down at the manicured fingernails digging into his flesh, and breathed deep. He didn't have anywhere near enough time for the careful thought and delicate consideration that this situation required—

Dixie shifted his weight forward, curled his toes back, and lifted his foot between the arch of Restano's thighs until it stopped against something solid. From the angle and velocity of his foot, Dixie assumed it was Restano's spine.

—Besides, he had wanted to do this ever since he met the man.

Restano released Dixie's arm, squeaked something high and Italian, and toppled over onto the gym floor.

The crowd gasped. There might have even been a few hoots and claps somewhere in the back, but Dixie didn't have enough time to stop and take a bow. The path to the stage was clear now, and he still had a message to deliver.

Dixie leaped up onto the stage, and though his adrenaline propelled him to clear the height with relative ease, it didn't much help with the landing.

He tipped forward, felt a marked increase in the airflow

on his nether regions, and heard an eruption of laughter from the audience.

Dixie straightened up and covered the breach with his hands. He had just presented his balls to his classmates. Dixie was pretty sure that this would damage his credibility as a public speaker.

He looked across the stage to Mark and the microphone in his hand. Mostly the microphone. He needed that. He didn't have anywhere near enough vocal capacity to scream over all that laughter.

"May I see your microphone for a moment, sir?" Dixie asked.

Mark didn't respond. He didn't seem capable of doing much besides staring and sweating. Evidently these kinds of stressful situations didn't pop up too often in AM radio.

Dixie lowered his shoulder and aimed at the man's gut. He had been hankering to hit something again, anyway.

He crashed into Mark's stomach and sent him staggering back across the stage. Luckily the homecoming queen cushioned his fall, so things turned out well enough for the man. Mark didn't look like he had much contact with attractive women that didn't require a fist full of singles and a two drink minimum.

Dixie picked the microphone up off the stage and turned to face the crowd. It was time to deliver his message to the people.

"Uhh . . ."

And were there ever a lot of them.

Dixie breathed in deep. He had once heard that some

people were more scared of public speaking than death. Obviously they had never shared a locker with a nudist linebacker.

"Rick Johnson has genital herpes and a cleft butthole."

Well, that part wasn't exactly true and didn't pertain to the investigation, but Dixie didn't expected to be let near a microphone in the near future and wanted to take full advantage.

A titter ran through the crowd that escalated into full-blown laughter. Dixie smiled; this was starting much better than he expected.

Someone screamed something high and ugly from beyond the stage.

Unfortunately that feeling didn't last too long.

Dixie looked in the direction of the noise: Rick hopped out of the shadows and moved toward the stage. He raised a crutch over his head like a war club, and cocked it back until his shirt popped free from its cummerbund.

It was at this moment that Dixie ran through some basic geometry:

Rick was six foot four with three-foot-long arms, swinging a four-foot club.

Dixie was five foot four, standing on a three-foot-high platform.

So, running through the Pythagorean theorem, that left Rick with more than enough room to gain momentum on the downward arc of his crutch swing before he collapsed Dixie's forehead.

This was bad.

Dixie crouched over and braced for the thud and the splash and the white lights and harps, but instead, he heard a grunt, then a groan, and then applause.

He looked up: Julie sat on top of Rick and tightened his neck in the vise between her bicep and forearm. Her dress was wrinkled and her makeup was smeared, but it didn't look like either was a result of the tackle.

"Go ahead and finish, Dixie."

Dixie looked down: Brandon stood in front of the stage and held the crowd at bay with one of Rick's crutches. He wore tuxedo pants, but nothing else. Evidently, he and Julie had made up. At least that would explain their mutual dishevelment and why he was too busy to claim his crown.

Dixie motioned to Julie. "She's a keeper."

"I know," Brandon said. "You better hurry."

Dixie nodded. Brandon was right. He only had one chance at this thing. It had to sound professional—

"Get off the stage!" Restano said in a hoarse croak as he unfolded himself from the fetal position and crawled up the stairs to the stage.

—And it had to be fast.

"There's meth in the football team! They bought the new field with drug money from selling bad crank to hoboes, and now they're smuggling it in from Canada!"

Dixie paused for breath and dramatic effect. There was no gasping or fainting in the audience. That's strange; Dixie was expecting plenty of both.

"You all get that?" Dixie asked.

Brandon looked up at the stage and shook his head in

the negative. So did everyone else in the front row. There might have been others, but things got a little blurry past the first few feet.

"Drop the microphone!" Restano crawled up the stairs, and Dixie edged to the far end of the stage. He didn't know if the man was motivated by professional responsibility or revenge, but he admired his dedication.

"Let's try this again." Dixie figured it was best to start out simple. This was a complicated scenario, and his audience was far too drunk and horny to comprehend much beyond a desire to rub their lower parts against something with complementary genitals. "Here's what we know for sure: Steve Funt and the rest of the football team are addicted to meth and have been using it as a performance booster all season."

The audience shuffled and murmured.

"A guy named Ralphino, possibly an alias, supplied the team with meth and paid for the new field by selling tainted drugs to the local homeless population."

Someone screamed something high and ugly, and Dixie weaved his head to avoid the empty bottle of schnapps that followed soon afterward. It wasn't quite the audience reaction that he was hoping for, but at least he had their attention.

"Now the football team's meth cartel has started smuggling in drugs from Canada and are gonna keep on killing hoboes and winning games unless we stop them!"

Funt pushed through the mass of people to the front of the stage, and the albino followed in his wake. Neither appeared as terrified or angry as Dixie expected, considering the circumstances. The empty bottle of schnapps was probably a factor.

"What the hell are you talking about?" Funt yelled, and the pleasant aroma of peppermint and diesel fumes drifted out of his mouth and up to the stage.

Dixie stepped forward into the disk of light on the stage. It was probably best that everyone saw him just then; he was pretty sure this was his dramatic moment.

"I've been onto you guys from the beginning," Dixie said, confident and clear. "You haven't made one illegal move that I haven't witnessed. I've entered your world, and I know your poison, and I'm not gonna let you ruin any more lives!"

"What?" The albino turned back to the crowd. "Is this kid retarded or something?"

Dixie sighed; he only had enough energy for the one dramatic moment, and they just had to go and screw with his momentum. "Guys, a little dignity, okay? It's over."

"I'm not a drug addict, you asshole!" Funt puffed out his chest and stepped toward the stage, but Brandon jabbed him with the crutch before he came any closer.

"Oh really? Dixie held the package over his head and pointed down at Funt. "Well, you sure do use a lot of drugs for someone who doesn't use drugs!"

The crowd gasped and Dixie smiled. So, he had one more dramatic moment left in him, after all. He imagined this would play great once he sold his life rights to ABC and they made this into a TV movie.

Funt pointed at the package. "That's my insulin."

"Sure," Dixie said. "Insulin, smack, crank . . . they're your drugs, call 'em what you want."

"No, I'm diabetic."

"Yeah, well lot's of people lose weight the healthy way," Dixie said. "You don't need the drugs."

"My body can't break down glucose, you idiot."

"What? You mean like B.B King?" Dixie closed his eyes and tried to shake out the realization that was creeping through his mind. "No, no way! That's a bluff! Does anyone have a pound cake?"

Dixie felt something grab his ankle and looked down: it was Restano.

"Stop . . . right . . . now."

"Dang." The package slipped out of Dixie's fingers and fell to the stage. That was okay. He didn't need it. Not anymore.

The syringe was full of insulin, not meth. The football players weren't crank heads, just natural-born sadists. The Canadian company wasn't smuggling narcotics, just importing reasonably priced pharmaceuticals.

Rick was still an asshole.

And it all made a whole lot of sense.

Chapter 31

Despite the public nudity, rampant slander, and kicking his principal in the groin, no formal charges were brought against Dixie. He assumed that the offended parties didn't want the official involvement to interfere with their own designs for suitable retribution. However, when the police arrived, they still decided it was best for everyone to take Dixie into custody.

Dixie understood their decision, and appreciated the protection, but still felt that the handcuffs were a bit excessive. He wasn't dangerous. He wasn't a flight risk. Not anymore. Not without the story.

He shifted his weight against the hard wooden bench in the lobby of the police station, and tried to find an angle where the paper toga didn't venture up into his unmentionables. No luck. Dixie made a mental note to ask for one of those orange jumpsuits or a hemorrhoid pillow the next time one of the officers walked by. He had experienced all manner of wedgie in his life, but there was none to compare with the sheer pain and irritation of the paper variety.

Of course, Dixie was willing to put up with the inconvenience or anything else to keep him from his parents for a little longer. Recent bonding notwithstanding, he didn't expect the sergeant to give much leeway where public nudity was concerned, and Dixie hoped that somebody had the foresight to prepare him for the news with a bottle of scotch.

Mostly, Dixie just appreciated the quiet to piece together the night's events. There was a lot that got shot his way in a short period of time and mostly in screams and threats, but from what Dixie could gather:

1. Funt was not a meth addict, just a diabetic, and the syringe that Dixie took from the trash can was used for injecting insulin, not meth.

2. This insulin was delivered to Funt, at a significant discount, from a company in Canada.

3. Funt had to inject the insulin in his buttocks, due to arm soreness from weight lifting.

4. The albino, Funt's friend and participant in the school's vocational nursing program, volunteered to help with the injections.

5. The "tainted shit" going around the football team wasn't bad narcotics, but mononucleosis from an especially involved fan named Heather.

6. Daniel Ralphino was not a meth kingpin, but rather, a noted philanthropist and could not attend the football game because he was distributing medicine in the Congo.

7. The Sudafed was used for this charity.

8. There was absolutely no connection between any of this and the overdoses in the woods.

9. Dixie was an asshole.

That last one didn't require much investigation. He was an asshole. And a bad reporter. There never was a meth cartel, just some chubby kid with diabetes, a generous old man, and some loosely tied coincidences. The week had been a total waste.

Well, maybe "total waste" was a bit harsh. He did get to kiss a cheerleader, break Rick's foot, and kick Restano in the junk, and any week he got to cross three items off his list of life goals couldn't be all bad.

Plus, since there weren't any laws against insulin possession, VisionQuest probably wouldn't be much of a concern when he went to the hearing on Monday. That was a relief. Dixie had already endured enough character building during the past week to last him for the foreseeable future.

So, all that left was riding out the consequences and punishments at home and school for the next few months. Dixie was pretty sure things would make their way back to normal before too long. Heck, by the time spring break was over, he doubted anyone would even remember his name, let alone that he stabbed Dale with a syringe, set the chemistry lab on fire, and flashed his testicles at the homecoming dance.

Well, except maybe Rick. He would still be in a walking cast, and it's pretty difficult for a person to lose track of a detail like that. Dixie figured it was best to give him some space. At least for the rest of their natural lives. That should be enough.

"Wait in here."

He looked up: a female officer steered Brynn by her hand-cuffed wrists to the bench and sat her down next to Dixie.

Dixie smiled. If he had known to expect visitors, he wouldn't have dressed so informally. He looked down to make sure that the paper covered his testicles. He didn't want Brynn to think he was immodest.

"Hi," Dixie said.

"Hi."

"You want to go first?"

Brynn sighed. "I got caught shoplifting bras at the Wal-Mart."

Dixie nodded. "Bummer . . . So, did they let you keep any?"

"No." Brynn looked up at Dixie and smiled. He was glad to see that incarceration hadn't broken her spirit, yet. "How about you?"

"Oh, just the same old thing."

Brynn laughed and tossed back the hair out of her face. She really did have beautiful eyes. It was a shame they didn't get out more often.

Dixie scooted across the bench until the flesh of his thigh bumped against the denim of Brynn's jeans. He squirmed against his handcuffs until his pinky found her.

"I missed you today."

Brynn grabbed Dixie's hand and held it tight. "Yeah, me too."

Dixie leaned his head against Brynn's shoulder and closed his eyes. Sure, there was pain and lies, bad whiskey and head trauma, public humiliation and nudity, police records and angry jocks, and he lost the story of his life, but at least he found a friend.

And maybe it wasn't such a bad week, after all.

Acknowledgments

I would like to thank my friends, family, and teachers for their support and encouragement.

Jennifer Besser and the fine folks at Disney-Hyperion.

Steven Malk and all the wonderful people at Writers House.

And most of all...

You. Thanks for buying my book. Seriously, that was awesome.

About the Author

While writing *Sophomore Undercover*, Ben Esch slept on a foldout sofa in his parents' basement, gained thirty pounds, and developed a crippling fear of raccoons. The author did not date much during this period.

Ben now lives in Los Angeles and sleeps in an actual bed. Chase your dreams, kids.